# i loved you, logan mcgee

## *also by irene bennett brown*

*Skitterbrain*

*Run From a Scarecrow*

*To Rainbow Valley*

*Willow Whip*

*Disobedience*

*Morning Glory Afternoon*

# i loved you, logan mcgee

IRENE BENNETT BROWN

WISE WOLF BOOKS
An Imprint of Wolfpack Publishing
wisewolfbooks.com
701 S. Howard Avenue 106-324
Tampa, FL 33609



This book is a work of fiction. Any references to historical events, real people or real places are used fictitiously. Other names, characters, places and events are products of the author's imagination, and any resemblance to actual events, places or persons, living or dead, is entirely coincidental.



Cover design by Wise Wolf Books

eBook ISBN 978-1-957548-46-3
Paperback ISBN 978-1-957548-81-4

*For Bobby Shannon, wherever you are,*

*& that other Bobby, too.*

# i loved you, logan mcgee

# one

If our school's guest speaker, chattering away up front, said "love" one more time, I was going to be sick. Our Valentine's Day treat, Maggie Austin, wrote teen romance novels. With each "love," she reminded me that Logan McGee was under the stupid impression that he and I ought to break up. My heart was beating: No way, no way, no way.

For six weeks he had been a bigger part of my life than my mom and dad, and little brother and sister. Besides, Logan himself had said, "Forever."

"Although Dirk was totally wrong for her, my character took on a fascinating new dimension when she fell in love with him..."

"Guh." I clutched my midsection.

"Calla, what's wrong?" Taking her attention from the speaker, my friend Emmy Voss nudged my elbow and whispered, "Are you sick or something?"

I barely glanced at Emmy's pale face. She's often taking medicine or vitamins for her anemia and is an authority on illnesses. But she is thirteen, like me, with no more experience with a broken heart than I have had. No way did I want her, or anybody, to know about mine. "I'm okay. Touch of flu, maybe." I hoped she was convinced. I admit to being creative and a fair actress, but I'm not into outright lying.

"Will you guys shut up!" My other friend, Rina Reynolds, hunched forward on the other side of me. "This is good stuff" and I can't hear."

You do what Rina commands. I wrapped my arms tight around me, clamped my lips, and prayed to last until the presentation was over. I should have skipped, faked the flu, gone home the minute I got Logan's goodbye note. The trouble was, I'm a wimp who normally doesn't have the guts to do such things—stuff that would only get me into more trouble.

I tried to concentrate on the author's looks, instead of on what she was saying. She was pretty, wearing a bright red dress and earrings that sparkled from the overhead lights when she moved her head. I was glad she was attractive. I want to be a writer, too, a playwright. It wasn't true, what some kids thought, that only ugly introverts could be successful writers. I was as outgoing as the next kid. Well, almost. Lots of people said I was cute. Logan McGee had, although today he was treating me like a warthog or something. Maybe he'd rather I wore my brown hair in curls instead of the French braid. Maybe I was too thin; my eyes too big and dark. I could pluck my brows...

I sneaked a look at Logan sitting a few rows ahead with his friend Teddy Marks. My eyes stung. Most everybody considered them the two cutest boys in Treebrook Middle School, which they were. Just looking at Logan's back made me feel dizzy; my throat dried. Normally, Logan would be sitting with me, like Shiney was sitting with Rina on her other side.

Rina's boyfriend, David Malone, is called Shiney by everybody because that's what he is—shiney. He's got big blue eyes that shine, perfect teeth that shine, and his complexion looks polished. At least that's why I always thought he had the nickname, but Rina said he got it originally from outshining everybody else at sports. If I was his girlfriend I'd prefer to think that, too.

Did kids notice that Logan wasn't with me? My heart hammered as I remembered the first day I saw him, during Christmas vacation, just past. Nothing like him had ever happened to Treebrook. Nothing so wonderful as Logan McGee had ever happened to me, Calla Lea Stafford, either.

. . .

I was walking home along Harlan Avenue from the senior citizen center where I do volunteer work, mostly directing skits. Thirteen may be young to be a director but I'll do anything for experience toward becoming a playwright, and coaching those people in little plays is a hoot. It was a cold day, and I stopped in at Happy Hank's Hamburgers for a hot chocolate.

A kid and a small lady, probably his mother, sat in the booth across from me. I'd never seen either of them before, because I definitely would have remembered the boy! I wondered if they were in Treebrook to visit over Christmas break. They stared back at me, talking. Did I have a marshmallow-and-chocolate mustache and were they short of things to talk about? I wiped my napkin across my hot face.

Out of the corner of my eye I watched the woman reach across the table to push the kid's arm. When he caught me staring in curiosity he glared at his mom, but it didn't do any good. I ducked my head a little, dying to know what was going on. Both of them had the same sandy-colored curly hair, high cheekbones, and big eyes. She continued to push and nod and yammer and smile sweetly at him. The next thing I knew he was on his feet, ambling toward my table!

My heart about quit. I gulped hot chocolate and coughed. Normally, a kid dressed like him wouldn't have impressed me in the least; he could have walked out of one of those TV Western reruns. He'd left his cowboy hat in the booth, but from his blue shirt, big silver belt buckle, and Levi's, down to his cowboy boots, he looked natural. Like he was from the real West—Wyoming, Texas, or Montana, not Oregon, where you don't see many regular cowboys. Maybe because he was different from Treebrook guys, who live in jeans, polo shirts, and tennis shoes, as alike as peas, that he suddenly appealed to me. Treebrook kids would have looked nerdy dressed like him, but he looked wonderful.

I got control of my flyaway emotions, stopped coughing, and looked up. A pair of hazel green eyes looked at me funny from the pink glow of his face. He rubbed nervously at the curls above his left ear. "I'm sorry. Mom made me come over here."

"It's all right. What does she want?" My own face blazed. But I felt sorrier for him. His mom swung her arm, like a small Napoleon forcing a charge, whenever the kid looked back toward their table.

"My name is Logan McGee and I'm from Texas," he said fast. No more than that, and the warm feelings already begun inside me churned more furiously. My face felt stiff with a weak grin, so different from how I really felt inside, where there was a huge smile for him.

"Hi, Logan. I'm Calla Lea Stafford. From right here. Treebrook, Oregon." I placed the flat of my hand on top of my cup, almost tipping it over. "Cl-clumsy," I stammered, but Logan gave me a slanty, comforting smile that dismissed my klutziness. I grinned at him, for real. "Are you visiting somebody in Treebrook?" Suddenly I wished deeply that he was visiting me, or someone I knew. Not my best friends Rina and Emmy, though. Rina has her own boyfriend, Shiney, but she is still a great-looking brunette, if you overlooked the dark hairs on her arms. Emma is the kind of pale blonde boys opened doors for. We've been best friends since second grade, but for sure I didn't want either of them for competition over Logan McGee from Texas.

"Not visiting," he shook his head. He went on in a soft drawl, "Mom and I just moved here. I'll be a midyear transfer to Treebrook Middle School. Mom says you probably go there, from the looks of your age— do you?"

I nodded. "Eighth grade. I'm thirteen." I was proud of the calm I showed on the outside, because somewhere in my head I was doing a gleeful jig for the miracle of this neat boy about to come to my school.

"Ask your friend to join us," the little Napoleon lady called out suddenly from their table. "Ask her over, Logan, honey."

Logan-honey looked practically purple. "Mothers!" he drawled just for my ears, making me feel special. "Sometimes I wish mine would pick clovers in front of a cattle stampede."

I laughed. "They can be a pain, all right."

His hazel-eyed gaze fastened to the center of my forehead. "Do you want to come over to our table, bring your stuff?"

"Nah, I don't think so." I looked at the brown dregs in my cup. "I'm almost finished and I should be getting home." Really, who wanted to go home?!

When Mrs. McGee saw I wasn't moving, she grabbed their plates and Coke glasses and hurried over. She smiled as she put the stuff down. I held my breath, not knowing what to do. She slid into the booth and motioned Logan to sit next to her. He rolled his eyes like he was praying for that stampede, making me want to laugh, but he sat down. I waited for her to say something, because for sure this was Mrs. McGee's scenario.

"This nice girl doesn't mind our butting in," she said to her son. "Do you—what's your name, hon? I'm Carole McGee, but just about everybody calls me by my nickname, Trinket. Don't have to tell you why."

I shook my head to show that I didn't mind. "I'm Calla Lea Stafford." Trinket McGee was like a toy person, but her steady expression made me think she was somebody who knew what she wanted and would go after it. I was curious to know what she wanted of me.

"We're new in town; maybe Logan told you." She tapped a pink fingernail against the side of her glass, and her light green eyes locked with mine. "I want so much for things to work out for Logan and me, here. I'm a secretary, and I initiated the transfer from Amarillo's Sun-Corn Tortilla Chip factory to the division plant here in Treebrook. To get far away from Texas." I waited, anxious to hear why, but she just sighed and for a moment played with the crumbs on her plate.

"Logan will tell you he's good and mad at me for making him leave Texas, his daddy's ranch," she said finally, giving Logan a look that pleaded for understanding and, probably, forgiveness. "But I had to get him out of there, before he got killed, too." I murmured questioning sympathy, because she wasn't being really clear if her husband had just died, or what. She went on: "Lo thinks he'd like to ride in rodeos like his daddy."

"Don't talk about Dad like he's dead," Logan drawled in a flat, stubborn voice. "You're only divorcing." I was glad he set things straight, even if it was mostly mad talk at his mom.

"No, but Thad's been hurt enough times and—so have you. Your father lives in constant risk of his life." She muttered under her breath, as if to herself. "And rodeoing isn't the only bad habit that will probably shorten his life." For a second she didn't say anything, just looked like she was trying not to cry.

I felt like I was eavesdropping on personal matters I shouldn't hear, but the McGees had moved to my table, not the other way around. Still, I was about to say that I'd better go when Trinket McGee looked at her son, her green eyes teary. "I don't want that for you, Logan. I want a lot better for you. You're a nice bright, caring boy—he gets A's," she said to me, her worried expression changing to a proud smile.

Logan tore a French fry into several pieces and then mashed them with his fork on his plate. I was certain the pieces were named: M-O-T-H-E-R. I felt for them both. No kid likes his mother to brag about him in front of another kid. But even if she hadn't told me, I could tell that Logan was special, not just any old boy from Texas.

"When Logan starts school next week I'd like for him to know someone who can help him make the adjustment. I know it's hard—new school, new faces." She spoke to Logan but he frowned into space, ignoring her.

I was beginning to see where I came in. "I'd be glad to show you around," I told Logan breathlessly. "I can introduce you to some of the kids before then."

"See there, see how easy it is." Mrs. McGee

looked happy with me. "Everything is going to turn out all right, Logan. You have a new friend, and we just got to town. Calla—what's your last name again?—Stafford, where do you live, hon?"

I told her. "Well, Logan can find it," she nodded. "You two can walk to school together and things like that. Right?"

"Sure," I said.

"Mom, maybe she doesn't want to..." Logan began.

"Oh, but I do. It's okay, really." My face heated up again. I could hardly wait to show him off, especially to Rina and Emmy. They'd die!

I'd totally lost contact with the speaker up front as I recalled that—for a kid used to being tossed from wild horses and getting his bones broken—Logan was timid the first few weeks in Oregon. Oh, he was cocky, sometimes, and cute, laughing at his own craziness. Plain to anybody he was covering up anxiety. At school he stayed so close to me, the other kids started taking it for granted we were a couple!

Now I slid down in the auditorium seat, feeling warm as I remembered back to about a month ago and the time he kissed me. Cartoons were on TV at my house that Saturday morning. The kids, Addie Marie and Hans, were stretched out on the carpet on their stomachs, eyes glued to the noisy set and "Spider-Man." Logan and I sat on the couch, our hands almost touching under the People magazine we were looking at together.

"Let's get out of here," Logan whispered, "and go to the Big Freeze for ice cream cones."

"Why are we whispering?" I whispered back.

He eyed my brother and sister on the floor. "Because I've only got a dollar. I don't want the little kids to get mad at me because I can't buy them ice cream."

I nodded. We slipped out like villains escaping Spiderman and, laughing, raced three blocks to the Big Freeze. Logan paid for a double-double fudge for him, pralines 'n' cream for me. On the way home he stopped. Feeling that I'd lost him, I turned. He stood there on the sidewalk with a "light-bulb-coming-on" look on his face. "What's the matter?" I giggled, walking backward, pulled deep into the collar of my coat because the ice cream was making me colder.

"I want to make a toast." He lifted his ice cream cone.

"You dip," I laughed at him. "You don't toast with ice cream."

"But I want to. We have to. Right now." He hurried up to me, and, standing very close, he touched his double-double fudge to my half-gone pralines 'n' cream. "Forever," he said.

I wrinkled my nose at him, sure he'd lost his mind. "Forever, what?"

"Forever us. You've been great, helping me get used to stuff, but not acting like you own me. I want you to be my—girlfriend, not just my friend."

I could barely breathe. In spite of Logan's quirky grin, his voice grew serious. "There weren't any girls as pretty as you, even in as big a state as Texas." He leaned forward and his mouth hit the corner of mine. The second time he tried was better. The tender, sweet touch of his lips on mine almost made my heart burst. "Okay," I said, with what breath I could muster. We walked on, quieter than usual, our hands holding each other's tight.

What everybody already thought had come true! I was Logan's girl, his only girl! He wasn't so timid anymore, he made other friends, but Logan and I stayed together, skating at the mall, walking home from school together, and talking. Talking about all sorts of stuff, like how it was flat and dusty but great ranching country around Amarillo, compared to hilly, rainy Oregon. Secret stuff about things we liked, or were afraid of, or what made us mad.

"Dad isn't nearly the scum Mom makes him sound," Logan told me angrily one day. We were at the park. We'd abandoned our bikes and were sitting on the motionless merry-go-round, just talking.

"How come they don't get along, then?" I asked, my eyes on two bundled little kids zipping down a slide not far away.

Logan shrugged. "I guess he plays around. You know, other women. But everybody likes him! He's the best bareback rider in Texas. We had a den full of rodeo trophies. Three shelves of them were mine, from roping calves and stuff. Some were from showing El Cabrillo."

I smiled sympathetically, hoping to rid Logan of his unhappy frown, as he scuffed at the gravel under our feet. I'd heard about his horse, El Cabrillo, before. His father had paid twenty thousand dollars for the animal. But when Trinket and Logan left Texas, she gave orders for Thad McGee to sell El Cabrillo because Logan wouldn't be riding and he would eventually need money for college. That had really made Logan mad!

Logan pushed off with his boot, and the merry-go-round started slowly to turn. I pulled my knees up and clasped my toes. "I don't know much about horses, but I think they are beautiful."

He slid closer and placed his arm around my shoulder. "Someday I'll teach you to ride." The park trees whirled by us as he made the merry-go-round go fast. He held me tight so I wouldn't fall off. Me, the happiest person on earth. Dreamer that I am, since about fifth grade I'd fantasized that my first love would come into my life a handsome knight on a white horse. Here it had happened almost the way I'd dreamed it. Logan had had to leave his horse when he came here but for sure he was the gallant knight kind. Nobody had treated me so special before.

Soon after, I got up the nerve to tell Logan about the stack of one-act plays I'd written over the last two years.

"Hey, can I read them?" We were in my room, looking for tennis rackets. My plays were in the bottom drawer of my desk, but I shook my head. "They aren't that good. Just practice. But maybe I'll let you read the three-act play I'm working on, when it's finished. I'm getting better, I think, since I saw three nationally known plays in Portland. I learned a lot from the sets, the acting, all of that."

"I've never known a girl who could write a real play! Listen, maybe we'll both end up in New York someday—I'll come to see your play on Broadway, and you can come watch me ride the broncs at Madison Square Garden!"

I looked at him, loving him so much, glad that we both had pretty big imaginations. One of us might have made fun, if one had been a dreamer and the other not.

For six wonderful weeks we were a close, perfect pair. I didn't own any cowboy boots, but I started wearing my short, cuffed suede boots with my jeans so I'd look more Western, like Logan.

Going around with Logan, I didn't see as much of my friends as I'd used to. Both Rina and Emmy behaved a little snitzy but claimed they were glad I'd got such a neat boyfriend. Then, Rina began to hint that she and Shiney might break up. I wasn't so blind that I missed her dreamy stare at Logan when she said that!

My mind came back to where I was, and I couldn't help glaring at Rina, beside me, staring in a dream state at the speaker on the stage. I listened to the writer say something about "greetings of love being passed in the month of February since the Middle Ages." That word, "love," again, was a jolt reminding me that inside the notebook on my lap was the valentine Logan had passed to me in the hall this morning before classes.

The front of the valentine said: YOU'RE SOMEBODY SPECIAL, and inside: SPECIALLY TO ME. HAPPY VALEN¬TINE'S DAY! Nothing great. In fact, it would have been just as suitable for him to give to Teddy Marks. But Logan's note, a small folded square inside the valentine, had hurt the most. It was a bomb!

"I want to be your friend, always," he had scribbled, "but not go steady anymore." Reading it, I felt tricked; I felt dumped like garbage. God, it had only been six weeks and he'd said forever! "Thank you for helping me get used to the new school, but," he wrote, "I want to spend more time with the guys, now that I've gotten acquainted. I might go out for weight lifting and track. So I won't have much time to spend with you, with any girl. P.S. I'll still like girls, but not one-to-one. P.P.S. I've thought about this a lot."

Thought about breaking up a lot? And I hadn't had a clue? Maybe I had never been as important to Logan as I'd thought. Because breaking up had been the farthest thing from my mind! The liar—I hated him. No, I loved him, but he couldn't do this to me. Not on Valentine's Day—what a stupid time to break up with a girl. Sir Logan had slipped on the gallantry scale this time. He couldn't dump me, he just couldn't, not ever. I choked on tears I had to keep back. On either side of me, Rina and Emmy giggled at something the writer said and squirmed in their seats. Love, huh? Love stank. Love—hurt. It made people sick. The world would be better off without it.

I felt a sudden burning in my throat and bolted to my feet. Emmy grabbed my arm. I shook her loose, making a motion with my finger to my mouth that I was about to be sick. She nodded, looking puzzled but sympathetic. Rina took it all wrong, as usual. "So you think Maggie Austin is too gushy? Well, I don't, I love her books, I can't wait to read her new one—!" She grabbed my other hand. "Wait a minute. Don't leave!"

I pleaded in a choked voice, "Please, Rina!" pulled free, and darted down the aisle.

Behind me, I could hear Maggie Austin winding up her speech. There was a racket as kids jumped to their feet to hurry up front to talk to her and buy her books. Not me. I needed a bathroom, fast.

# two

I'd die if it was really over between Logan and me. In the empty restroom, I pushed my forehead against the cool mirror above the sink. The awful churning in my stomach was going away, but I wanted to be sure. And I wouldn't be alone long. Half the school combed their hair between classes.

I choked back sobs. "I love you, Logan McGee, I really love you. I can't give you up!" Hearing my own words out loud made them concrete, made me feel that somehow he didn't really mean what he'd written. Possibly we'd be back together by this afternoon. I wiped my eyes.

"Calla, you in here?"

Before answering Emmy, I ducked into a stall and quickly tore Logan's note into bits and flushed it noisily down the toilet. "Yeah, I'm here." It made me mad that my voice sounded queer. I hoped she wouldn't ask anything. Grade-school breakups were simpler and, in a way, fun. You told your friends, snubbed the boy, and liked someone new by the next day. But it wasn't like that anymore.

Girls poured in, the restroom door thumping in and out as though shoved by their shouts. Ordinarily, I would be laughing and talking with the rest, but suddenly, listening from the stall, I was reminded of noisy geese and couldn't stand any of them. I wanted desperately to get through the door without anybody asking questions about Logan and me. I blotted my eyes again with a square of tissue, took three deep breaths, smoothed the hair at my temples, and arranged my single braid over my shoulder. I pushed out of the stall into the crowded room, head down, hoping I could get out without either Emmy or Rina catching me.

Somebody's elbow jabbed me in the ear. It hurt, but before I could tell the girl off, a blue skirt parked in my path. "Cal, look, I bought three of Austin's paperbacks!" Rina gushed in my face. "Toni and Jerry, Bound by Love, and There's Always Tomorrow. Aren't you just thrilled? God, she signed them! They're autographed, to me. And to Shiney. I told Maggie Austin to put his name down, too."

"Great," I mumbled. I wanted to keep going, but

Rina would ask why. So I just stood there casually, with my feelings tight inside and ready to blow.

"I can't believe you didn't buy any books," Rina went on. "I would have loaned you the money. Paperbacks don't cost so much, and God, I mean, they're autographed."

I nodded. Gritting my teeth to keep from saying something I'd be sorry for, I pushed between two seventh graders and pretended to check my lipstick in the mirror. I looked so awful I wanted to die. I wondered if I could get legitimately excused to go home. Then I saw Emmy's pale, lightly freckled face over my shoulder, studying me intently in the mirror. Nosy-body. Why did she have to see everything? She should mind her own business. "Gotta go." I squeezed and shoved my way toward the door.

"Wait, Calla!" Rina ordered, hurrying up behind me as I went out into the hall. "What's her big rush, Em? Cal is sure behaving like a ditzo today." Emma shushed her, but Rina went on, "I mean, what's wrong with you, Cal? For weeks you've been crazy about the idea of Maggie Austin coming to talk to us about her romance novels on Valentine's Day. We all were. But I don't think you even listened to her presentation. Then you ducked out and didn't go up front with us to meet her, or anything. That was your idea originally, remember? You were just wild at the prospect of talking to a real author about writing. You said you might even show her one of your plays—"

She was right. But that was before Logan's note demolished me and my morning. Curiously, Maggie Austin and writing were now unimportant to me. I shrugged.

"Calla's sick, aren't you?" Emmy said in her soft voice. "Or is something else the matter?" I had to look away from the concern on her face.

"She can't be that sick," Rina persisted. "I mean, you're walking upright, Cal, and you don't look sick. You do act funny, though. Like you lost your best friends." She giggled. "But we are here, right on your butt."

"I wish I could," I snarled before I could stop myself.

"Hey, she's talking to us," Rina laughed. "Wish you could what?"

I whirled around and faced them, feeling the blood rush to my face. "I wish I could lose you." I sounded hateful. But it felt so good to say something nasty to somebody that I wasn't sure I wanted to stop. I stared at them, breathing hard, just waiting for one of them to say something, anything, so I could spit out more mean words, lots of them.

"Calla Lea Stafford, why are you talking to us like this? What's gotten into you?" Rina stared at me, her upper lip beginning to twitch as her temper flared.

"Maybe you'd feel better if you told us what's wrong," Emmy added.

"It's none of your business! You're such a snoop, Emmy Voss. You'd love to have some gossip to spread all over school, wouldn't you?" Even though I'd never known Emmy to spread rumors, I was suddenly convinced she'd love to tattle that Logan wanted to dump me.

"Emmy isn't a snoop and you know it, Calla. She's just trying to be nice."

"Nice? So, who needs nice? Why don't you two just leave me alone?" I turned on my heel, clutching my notebook tight to my chest to halt the quivering that was overtaking me again.

"We will leave you alone!" Rina shouted after me. "Who needs you? You're some friend, Calla. You don't have to be so bitchy."

"Yes, I do," I laughed harshly over my shoulder at them.

"This isn't like you at all, Calla. Please tell us what's wrong," Emmy tried again in a horrified voice.

I whirled back. "Nothing. I'm just a bitch, remember? Ask Rina, the hairy orangutan." All three of our mouths dropped open, mine first. I'd never stooped so low to get back at anyone. And Rina was my friend. I felt sick inside, disliking myself, the horrible way I was suddenly behaving. It wasn't all my fault, though, I decided; it was partly theirs for pestering me. I started running down the hall, dry-eyed, my head aching. I'd lost Logan. And now, because of my big mouth, my very best friends would never speak to me again.

The rest of the afternoon was ghastly. Rina and Emmy avoided me. I caught Logan watching me out of his wide, hazel-green eyes during social studies class. But, when I attempted a smile he turned red and got very interested in his textbook. A definite act; I know for a fact that Logan gets A's without hardly ever cracking a book. After school I stayed by my locker for a while, my feelings taut as I listened for the sound of his boots to come tapping down the hall as he looked for me to say he was sorry and had changed his mind. For a long time I waited, tears gathering in my throat until I felt I'd suffocate, but he didn't show.

The world was ending and I couldn't stop it, I thought later, as I started up Grant Street toward home, alone. The sun that had been out earlier had gone; the air chilled the tears on my face. I couldn't ever go back to school, of course. No way could I face Rina and Emmy after what I'd said. And I'd rather die than be in the same school with Logan, knowing he didn't want to go with me anymore.

Maybe I could get a tutor and stay home? I could take over the housework, and Mom wouldn't have to get a babysitter for Addie Marie and Hans while she was at her job at the florist shop and Dad was at the post office where he is postmaster. A reasonable, excellent plan. I half wished I could offer it to Mom. But I knew she'd say I was having "another, totally impossible flight of fancy." She killed some of my very best ideas with that remark.

I hadn't realized I'd turned the corner west onto our street, Conser, until I heard a voice call out cheerfully, "Hello, Calla Lea." I looked up. Mrs. Van Heusen stood with tall, old Mr. Dabler on the sidewalk in front of her apartment. Quite a few of the senior citizens whom I worked with at the center lived in this low-income apartment complex named Conser Arms. Numb from the day's happenings, I just stared back at the two of them for a minute. Mr. Dabler's smile would melt an ice floe ordinarily. But I just waved and hoped it would do. No way did I feel like conversation.

Mr. Dabler didn't seem to notice. "Happy Valentine's Day," he called. "Happy day of love—sweetheart," he added with emphasis, teasing. I nodded, managing to grin back at him for a few seconds before I continued on. "Dear Old Dabler" Mom called him. He was a cute character; he wore faded Nikes with his worn suits and made rounds to the town taverns every day like clockwork. Not to go in, though. Mr. Dabler went to pick up whatever change might have fallen from people's pockets on the sidewalk outside the taverns. His "butter-and-egg" money, he called it.

"Don't forget Saturday," Mrs. Van Heusen's voice floated thinly after me. I turned and walked backward a bit, smiling as best I could, and waving. Then I turned around, my heart heavy inside me. Happy day of love? What a joke! What a bad joke. And I was supposed to help my elderly friends with a Valentine's Day skit on Saturday. I'd be dead by then if I didn't come up with a way to smooth things between Logan and me.

I just couldn't accept the reasons he'd given me in the note, for breaking up. There had to be a problem, hopefully minor. If so, I'd take care of it right away, because I couldn't stand the awful way I felt.

When I got home I'd have an onion sandwich, I decided, a treat I like anytime, but especially when I'm depressed. I didn't care that Dad says it's unattractive for a person to eat onion sandwiches the way I do. I like them. And I don't think they are any more unattractive than the tiny little cucumber sandwiches the senior citizens serve at their "tea parties"—those sandwiches that get the whole crowd to burping and patting their middles, practically in unison.

Logan didn't believe I liked onion sandwiches

when I first told him and fixed him one. He laughed and laughed and thought I was crazy as a loon, although he said he liked French onion soup. Maybe Logan minded onion breath more than he let on? When I think about it, Dentyne chewing gum commercials are pretty convincing when they show TV viewers that bad breath can lose you a person you like. I would have thought it would have to be more than that to change Logan's mind about me, but maybe not. I could probably give up onion sandwiches, if it meant getting Logan back. I felt guilty and a little foolish as I wondered if onions were the problem. Maybe it was something small and silly like that. If so, I could definitely fix it. In fact, I'd do anything. Anything at all, to get him back.

I started to cry again, thinking that stuff like pizza and nachos gave a person bad breath, too. You couldn't give up eating altogether. The answer was to have tons of Dentyne around, I supposed. Somehow I had to get together with Logan and make him tell me why he wanted to break up, so I'd know if it was something small like bad breath, or something bigger.

When I got home, Mrs. Lakley, the babysitter, stood ready to leave, with her coat already on. The wild expression in her eyes and her messed-up hair told me that the kids had driven her nuts again. Addie Marie and Hans sat side by side on the couch as though tied there by invisible ropes. Proving that Lakley had gotten tough with them. Not that I cared to know for what— I had enough problems of my own. I didn't say anything to any of them, just went for the stairs.

You don't get by Mrs. Lakley that easy, though, if she doesn't want you to. "Calla!" she said crisply, "just a minute, please." I turned as slowly as I could, dropping one shoulder and sighing loudly, to show her I didn't welcome the interruption. She ignored that and, gripping the front doorknob, said through stiff lips, "You can tell your mother or not, but those two were a handful and then some today." She motioned toward the brown-haired, angel-faced imps that Mom and Dad had seen fit to add to our family in the last few years, although God knows why. Addie, who is five, put her arm around our three-year-old brother's shoulder. Her bottom lip quivered and drooped when Lakley clucked her tongue and shook her head.

I gave Mrs. Lakley a half-smile and shrugged, wishing she'd go ahead and leave. I needed to go to my room and be alone. I guessed I'd have to hear what happened, though, before she'd ever turn that doorknob. "So what did they do this time?" I stared at a gilt-framed picture of pink roses that hung on the stairwell wall.

"They spit. They spit chewed-up raisins all over

the carpet. I like to never got it all cleaned up. I think they chewed up a whole pound boxful."

That was a casualty when I had Logan to worry about?! I looked at Addie. "Raisins?"

"We were playing baseball player."

"How do you figure? Why the raisins?"

"We pretended the raisins was that dark stuff the baseball players spit on TV," Addie explained.

Sometimes Addie is so inventive you almost have to admire her. I sighed. "You hit all the bases, then? With raisin chewing tobacco?"

Hans grinned. "Yeah."

"Dad's fault," I told Mrs. Lakley, hoping to satisfy her and hurry her off. "He never misses a baseball game that's televised. And the kids don't miss anything they see." Her expression said that was no excuse. "They pick up some pretty dumb ideas," I admitted. At that, she finally looked satisfied and she turned the knob; I thanked God.

Going out the door, she threw back, "Well, I just wanted you to know why they're being punished. I really shouldn't have to clean carpets; I wasn't hired to clean."

"No, Mrs. Lakley, I know you weren't. I'll tell Mom." I added grimly, "And they'll stay on the couch, and we'll see they get nothing but bread and water for dinner." She gave me a sharp look, decided it was a joke, and left with a pasted-on smile. In truth, I thought the bread and water was a good idea, if I could get Mom to agree. I was tired of their trouble—tired of everybody's.

"If either of you move, I'll kill you," I told Addie and Hans after the door had closed. "I'm going up to my room, and I don't want to hear a sound down here."

Han's little chin jutted out in protest, and Addie put her hands on her hips, wriggling there on the couch. "You're not the boss of us," she mocked.

"No, I'm your would-be murderer." I glared, then relented a little. "You can turn on the television. Then back on the couch and don't move a muscle. Or you know what will happen."

"We'll get killed!" Hans shouted gleefully.

"Right-o," I snapped. Normally, I'd have gone over and hugged him at that point, to show I was kidding, and explained to the little fool that getting killed wasn't exactly a fun thing to have happen to you. But this wasn't normal. My life had been pulverized; my head ached and all I wanted was to get away from everybody forever.

Upstairs, I sprawled onto my bed, the hurt inside me leaden and undissolvable—the worst feeling I'd ever had in my life. Behind my closed eyes, I saw again Logan sitting with Teddy Marks ahead of me at the author's talk. I jerked upward when I suddenly recalled that Lawrie Stamper had been sitting on Logan's other side. Stupid me! I hadn't realized she must have been there with

Logan the whole time. Our relationship wasn't even cold yet and he'd already found another girl? Lawrie, of all people?

Lawrie Stamper was a ditzo! Could that frizzle-headed sex bomb who'd had big boobs since fourth grade really have been with Logan? He wanted to break up because of sports with the boys, he'd said in the note. It was no fair; it was worse than I thought. I was as straight up and down as a stick—I had nothing to fight back at Lawrie Stamper with. I hated both of them!

I snatched a pillow from behind me and, without looking, heaved it at the wall. The resounding crash startled me. I saw that it was my chickens, my three shelves of collected chickens that I'd connected with. Damn the chickens, anyway, I thought in a fury, glaring at the mess of broken china and other stuff on the floor. They hadn't been my idea in the first place. Just because I flipped over a pair of stuffed chicks an aunt gave me when I was a baby, people started giving me chickens— in porcelain, ceramic, plastic, and stuffed.

Before I'd learned to express myself well enough to tell people I really didn't like chickens all that much, I'd been given nearly fifty of the stupid things! All the time I was little, the chickens took up space I'd rather have used for other things. When I told her, Mom said it was too late. It was best not to hurt my relatives' feelings. Another reason I kept quiet is that I've always been a superstitious person—about some things. Although I knew better, I couldn't help but feel that if the chain of incoming chickens was broken, I might have bad luck or something. So the chickens kept coming.

Now I'd broken a bunch of them. What did the chickens matter, anyway, though, when my whole life was already in ruins? I dragged myself over to view the damage, stooping to pick up a little red china rooster that had been decapitated in the crush. Aunt Ilene had given me the little red rooster for my sixth birthday. I caressed his broken neck with my thumb, feeling the rough edges. Poor little headless chicken. A knot started in my throat. A warm tear ran down my cheek, then the tears came in a flood, and the broken chickens got blurry. My fingers combed the broken mess for the missing head, and then I gave up. Oh, Logan, why? I threw myself on my bed and cried myself empty.

I must have fallen asleep. The next thing I knew Mom was screaming my name from the foot of the stairs. I recognized a mad scream, though, not a scared or worried scream. In the bathroom I splashed water on my face and gargled a capful of Scope to get the dead-mouse taste out of my mouth. I jabbed lipstick at my mouth and headed downstairs to see why Mom had her drawers in an uproar.

"What's the matter?" I asked, kind of surprised when I saw her coming up the stairs to get me.

"You're supposed to take care of the kids after Mrs. Lakley leaves!" I could see Mom was attempting to hold her voice down to a low yell. She stood on the stairs with one hand on her hip and the other about to twist the top button off her new greige, (that's grey and beige together), cotton shirt; her light blue eyes were furious.

"I was taking care of them," I protested, taking a couple of slow steps down. "Sort of. I told them to watch cartoons and not move from the couch."

"Well, they moved, they moved. The police came and pulled your little brother in off the street. He was marching up and down the block, stark naked. In February."

"It's not so cold—"

"Calla Lea Stafford, that is not the point. He could have been snatched by some weirdo. He's an innocent child, and he needs supervision at all times. " As usual, Mom put emphasis on the words she didn't want missed.

"I'm sorry." I probably looked as glum as I felt. "What was Addie doing when all this was going on? Why wasn't she making him behave?" I asked, hoping to shift a little blame if I could.

"She was into mischief of her own," Mom spoke

through her teeth. "Addie Marie took a twenty-dollar roll of postage stamps from my desk and pasted every last one of them into her Sticker Fun book."

"God."

"Yes, God. When I spanked her she wanted to know if it was for the box of raisins they chewed up and spit on the floor today, or the stamps, or both." Mom's long brown hair fell into her face as she shook her head. She looked tired.

I've always felt that my mother is an absolutely perfect candidate for a makeover. At that moment she looked in special need, dressed in that dull-colored shirt and jeans, and her makeup worn off. But I had no room to talk. We both must have looked pretty wrung out and awful, our resemblance a closer match than usual. Most of the time I take pains to look nice; Mom says she doesn't have time to primp and fuss, and it shows.

"Huh?" I realized she was still talking; I hoped she hadn't read my mind.

"I said, 'I've got them playing quietly with a puzzle in their room.' I want you in the kitchen to help with dinner. You can make a spinach-and-bacon salad and set the table, while I finish the beef casserole."

I hated for Mom to be so straight-out bossy, but she missed my frown as she went on. "I'm totally beat. Every man and his brother came in to buy flowers today. I wanted to get out and pick up a little Valentine's Day gift for your father, but there wasn't a chance. Poor guy. God knows, they had a rough day at the post office, too. He'll be happy, though, if we can just have a peaceful evening in front of the fire."

I followed her downstairs into the kitchen, ready to take commands like a robot—I felt so empty inside.

# three

Luckily, it didn't take much thought to fry the bacon crumbles and tear up spinach for the salad. I turned my mind to the valentine I'd given Logan first thing at school today —when I still believed he was mine. It was a heart-shaped apple that looked like a lace-trimmed valentine with stem and leaves. TO MY SWEET-HEART, it said. LOVE IS THE FRUIT OF FRIENDSHIP. And then on the inside: PLEASE BE MY DARLING VALENTINE, FOREVER. Feeling the way he did about us now, the Valentine had probably embarrassed him. Maybe he'd laughed at it. Or thrown it away. I felt sick.

"Hey, Bright Eyes!" Dad said as he came into the kitchen. He caught my shoulders in a one-armed hug, without looking at my eyes to know how they were. Since he literally smelled tired, I forgave him as he took his place at the table.

Mealtimes can be a noisy circus at our house, so I was just as glad at dinner that nobody really said anything. Mom and Dad drooped at their places and ate slowly. The little kids, whipped into shape for their nonsense, were behaving almost human. Of course, I was miserable over Logan. A bite of Mom's casserole stuck like a mudball in my throat. I couldn't help making faces as I got it past the painful lump in my throat. Mom didn't notice; otherwise, she would have killed me, thinking my hating her casserole was the big problem. Finally, I said a silent "to heck with it" and put my fork down to stay. I could hardly wait to leave the table.

Unfortunately, Dad was beginning to perk up as his plate emptied. "Don't anybody move until you see my Valentine's Day surprise!"

He whipped over to the refrigerator and came back with a frothy red-and-white dessert. It looked a lot like the Valentine I'd given Logan. I swallowed hard; the dessert got blurry. I blinked a few times.

"The mail was so heavy today I nearly lost my zip," Dad said, winking at me, "but I still drove into Portland to pick up this little baby at a French pastry shop."

Maybe the "zip" joke was cute, but I couldn't smile. Dad looked disappointed, which made me feel even worse. I like my father; we've always had a good relationship. When he's not tired he's a very smiley person—and good-looking. He reminds me of the guy who plays the lead in "Three's Company" reruns on TV; some-thing-or-other Ritter is his name. Except I think Dad is older. He's thirty-eight, four years older than Mom. Also, his hair is darker than the Ritter guy's and getting a little thin on top.

I ate a few bites of dessert and then carried my dish to the dishwasher before Dad could see that I hadn't finished. To make it look good, I began scraping and rinsing cooking utensils and adding them to the dishwasher, too. I caught Mom's smile of surprise and relief. I might have felt good if I'd been doing the work for any reason but to get out of there.

"You've been awfully quiet, sweetie," Dad said to my back, in a moment or two. "And you didn't take to the chocolate torte like I pictured you would. I thought you'd be on seconds by now. Bad day at school? You got a problem we need to discuss?"

"Sure," Mom looked up, as I turned around. "We're never too tired to talk over a problem if you need us, Callie. I doubt that the scolding I gave you for not watching the kids is making you look so down. What's the trouble?"

I stared at them through burning eyes. Then, suddenly I straightened and swallowed tears that threatened. No way was I going to tell them that Logan didn't like me anymore! I was going to fix things up, so it really wasn't over. I faked a grin. "No problem," I lied in a voice that wasn't mine, either.

Mom and Dad exchanged a look. Not that their voices hadn't sounded caring enough, before. But I could see by their faces that they wanted to go and relax in front of the fire more than they wanted to get into any heavy discussion with me. "Really," I managed to sound more natural this time, "nothing's the matter." They nodded, and I got out of there a few minutes later, shoving the dishwasher's ON button on the fly.

In my room, I gave up on the chicken mess when I cut my finger on a broken piece of porcelain. Not wanting to go back downstairs and have my parents see me crying so hard, I stuck my finger in my mouth and hoped the bleeding would stop without a Band-Aid. I turned my radio up loud so they wouldn't hear me sniffling and began to gather everything Logan had ever given me into a pile on the bed.

Looking at them somehow brought him back to me. I hugged a stuffed striped tiger and a little pink pig in one arm. I'd told Logan the first time he came to my house my opinion of chickens and he'd never given me one. With my other hand, I touched a dried and flattened carnation to my wet nose. How good the flower smelled that other day at the mall, when

Logan bought it for me. Shiney Malone bought Rina one at the same time, but the whole idea, to buy them for us, had been Logan's. It was hard to see through my tears, but I managed to fasten on my wrist the silver chain bracelet he'd given me. It was my most favorite piece of jewelry ever.

Except maybe for the pull tab from the pop can that I now slipped on my finger. On the way home from the market one day, with stuff for Mom, Logan had put the circle of metal on my finger. "It's a promise ring," he'd said.

I shoved everything aside and lay back on the pillow.

Logan's Valentine's note was somewhere under the town in the sewer system, where it belonged! I couldn't blame Logan, though. Lawrie Stamper, fighting unfairly with a twenty-five-year-old full-blown figure on an age-thirteen body, had to be the cause of all this. I covered my streaming eyes with my arm. I'd love to wring her neck for coming between us. Logan couldn't really like such a ditzo. But even if he did, I'd win him back. I'd have to move fast, use special strategy. Knowing Lawrie Stamper, she was feeding him green M&M's. She was that kind. I stopped crying, sat up, and blew my nose.

The whole world knows that some college girl did a research paper on what turns people on to love and found that green M&M's really did the trick.

I remembered that a couple of girls at our middle school, Kendra Farrell and Elizabeth Chelsea, tried it and had boys interested in them, even guys like Alex Barrington and Rick Mills. Nobody else actually saw this happen, but Kendra and Elizabeth swore on the name of the pope it was true. Miss Sheridan, our health teacher, overheard them talking, and she said M&M's wouldn't turn anybody on.

I sighed heavily. No matter how much she claimed she doubted it, I knew there was something to the green M&M's. Because Miss Sheridan called Elizabeth and Kendra into her office for a private lecture and made the rest of us sit through her film on human reproduction and birth control for the third time. She was worried, all right. Which was dumb. We wanted boys to like us, that was all.

No more tears, I decided. I stiffened my spine and lifted my chin in the way of a valiant actress facing a horde of attacking space aliens. Sitting around crying wasn't going to get me what I wanted: Logan. I had to take action. Affirmative action!

I got up, walked a bit, then went back to flop on the bed. I wished I could go out and buy pounds of M&M's and sort out the green ones. Did one person eat them, or did the couple eat them together, for them to work? And what reason could I give Mom and Dad for wanting to buy two pounds of M&M's? I really did need a subtle, elusive potion of some kind. I wanted Logan, like a dumb moth, to smash himself against an irresistible light bulb—me—after taking something. Oh, to make it happen!

I knew that several old people at the center swore by certain beliefs, potions, and so on. They knocked wood for good luck, planted their gardens by the moon's shape, and old Mr. Dabler talked all the time about how he kept a copper penny taped to his shoulder to ease his bursitis. Other people, like Miss Sheridan, might not believe in love potions, green M&M's, or whatever. But my own feelings about such stuff had always been that you never can tell.

I thought about a paperback novel I read one time. Mom would have killed me if she'd known I was reading it. The Southern belle in the story wanted this handsome guy, a plantation owner, to fall for her, I remembered. She made a potion from the web of a wild gander's foot, drying the foot and pounding it into a powder. She then put a pinch of this stuff into her dream man's coffee and the next thing she knew they were making love down in a bayou. I smiled to myself. It was about the most convincing thing I'd ever read.

Seeing things in print does make them hard to argue against, sometimes. The thought of books reminded me that in our basement was a book that was Grandma's. A very old book of home remedies like how to stop bleeding with cobwebs, or how to use flaxseed in a poultice to draw infection from a wound, or make herbal teas for endless ailments. But I remembered now, getting excited, that the book had recipes for love potions, too. I laughed when I read them in fifth grade, but I wasn't desperate, then. I didn't know I was going to fall in love with a boy like Logan and then lose him for no good reason.

I was opening my door to go to the basement when the phone rang.

"Cal," Mom called up the stairs, "it's Emmy Voss."

I closed my eyes, feeling dread, and then I yelled, "Got it!" I went back and flopped on the bed to talk on my phone. "Hi, Emmy." I held my breath, scared of what she might say.

Her voice, when she went on, sounded as worried as mine. "Calla, I just wanted to tell you if Rina and I did something wrong today, I'm sorry." I noticed she didn't say "we."

And how did this situation get reversed? Emmy hadn't done anything, but it was like her to apologize, anyway. "You didn't do anything, Emmy. It was all my fault. I didn't feel good and I kind of nipped. That's all, and I'm sorry."

"Then you're not mad?"

"No."

"And you're feeling okay?"

"Uh, better."

"Good. I was afraid you wouldn't come to my music program, and I really hoped you'd be there."

"I wouldn't miss it. It's tomorrow night, Friday, right?" It was sort of strange that Emmy Voss was a good friend. We weren't very much alike. She had a fabulous soprano singing voice. I sound like a sister to a bullfrog. I remembered that up to about sixth grade Emmy pestered me to take chorus with her. Then I did and, being friends, stood next to her to sing. She kept turning to stare at me, and the instructor did, too. After a week they both let me drop chorus with no argument.

"Is something funny?" Emmy asked suddenly in my ear.

"I was just thinking about sixth grade, Em, when I took chorus with you."

"Oh. If you're really interested, Callie, maybe you could take music lessons."

"Get serious! Maybe I'll write lines for a song, someday, but that's all."

In a few minutes, Emmy said she was glad we were still friends and hung up. As I replaced the phone on the hook I pictured her in the farmhouse where she lived. It was another odd difference between us that didn't matter. Emmy's parents owned a bean-and-poultry farm on the edge of town. They were older people, with old-fashioned ways that rubbed off on Emmy. But I liked her and I was glad she had called. Making up with Rina wouldn't be as easy, I knew. I wouldn't worry about it right then, though. Anxious to get on with my project, I hurried to the basement to find the big remedy book.

Back in my room, I saw that there was a lot of stuff in the book that wouldn't work for me. Like, I didn't have any cockleburs. I read that a girl could name a cocklebur for her lover, then throw it against her skirt. If it stuck, it meant her loved one was true, but if it fell off she might as well give up. I was half glad I didn't have any available cockleburs, whatever they were. I sure wouldn't want one falling off my skirt, proving for certain that Logan didn't like me.

Another charm, I read on, was to put a feather in your glove and just shake hands with the man you want. Not too difficult to pull off. But a couple of others—wearing a wasp's nest or the beard of a wild turkey gobbler hidden in my clothes—were completely out of the question. I was sorry, too, because the writer of the book swore either would make a man fall madly in love with you.

Finally, I found a suggestion I could use: Lemon

on a bedpost, according to the book, would make a man helpless to resist a girl. I didn't care how silly it sounded, I knew I had to try it. According to the directions, a person cut a lemon in half, rubbed the four corners or posts of the bed with both halves, then placed the halves under her pillow. In the night, if she dreamed of the guy, the book said, he was forever hers.

Great! I laid the book aside, refusing to let myself have any doubts. Maybe I could dream Logan back to me in a very strong dream. Maybe the invisible force of my dream would reach him like hypnosis and make him know how much I cared for him and him for me, really. I'd try it! Nobody needed to know—they'd just laugh.

This panicky feeling I had wasn't going to go away unless I did something definite about Logan and me right away. A little lemon on a bedpost wouldn't hurt anybody, and where was the proof that such a thing couldn't work, anyway? The book made it sound like strong stuff.

I slipped downstairs, feeling both confident and slightly insane. As I passed the living room I saw that Mom and Dad were cuddled together on the couch in front of the TV; asleep, I thought. In the kitchen I picked out four of the biggest lemons from the fruit basket on the counter and got a sharp knife from the knife block. I was all set and heading back up the stairs when Mom's voice stopped me. "Calla, where on earth are you going with that knife and those lemons?"

She was sitting forward, looking through the living room doorway at me. "Science project," I said quickly. "I'm going to make some mold."

"Oh, well, all right." Mom yawned and sat back. "Don't stay up much longer, though, Calla. We all need our sleep."

"Sure, Mom, I'm getting ready for bed now."

Strong as it was supposed to be, I still wanted to give the love potion lots of help. I took a bubble bath. In kind of a ritual before putting on my nightgown, I rubbed myself all over with some cologne Logan had given me. If I'd had some candles I would have lit them to help the magic work. I cut the lemons and rubbed the halves all over my bookcase headboard. My bed didn't have posts. I put the wrinkly lemon halves under my pillow, and, for extra power, I put a picture of Logan under my pillow with the lemons. Let people laugh if they wanted. I felt better, doing something. As I crawled into bed I knew the potion was going to work. Somehow, it would.

A couple of hours passed. The smell of cologne on me, and lemon on my bed, was powerful. I rolled around, half awake. Then the cologne smell started to fade and strong lemon remained, the winner. I thought of lemon drops and my mouth watered. I buried my nose in my blankets to block out the lemony smell, but it was like I was possessed by a demon. I felt starved, picturing lemon meringue pie and three-layered yellow cake with lemon frosting. I hadn't thought the mystical process would involve the torture I was going through.

Gradually, the loud growling of my stomach brought me more awake than ever. I sat up and punched my pillows to make my back comfortable, and turned on the lamp by my bed. Talk about stupid. This was stupid. This was crazy. There wasn't any magic, and the potion was backfiring on me. I was out of my mind! Lemon on my headboard wasn't going to make Logan fall back in love with me. I'd fooled myself for a while because I hurt and wanted Logan back so badly.

All the lemon was doing was keeping me awake, when I was dying to just fall asleep and forget everything. Stupid, stupid. But I left the lemon rinds under my pillow just in case. I rolled out of bed and got my social studies book from the floor. Reading a chapter in it would put me to sleep.

I couldn't concentrate with the smell of lemon filling my nostrils. I dropped the book and thought about the author presentation today. Too late, I wished I had bought a couple of Maggie Austin's books. Maybe they'd have had something in them that would have helped me deal with Logan. I just had to do all I could to make him like me again.

Finally I started to feel drowsy. Relieved, I turned off my light and snuggled down in my blankets, hopefully to go to sleep with a vision of Logan's slanty grin and adoring hazel green eyes on me. All I could see were lemons.

I must have fallen asleep because the next time I looked at my clock radio, the luminous green hands pointed to three ten. I felt raggedly tired, not rested at all. My stomach cramped with hunger worse than ever; that must have woken me up. I realized that the only way I could get rid of the cloud of lemon fragrance that still floated around me was to get up and wash my bed off. But I was too tired for that. Maybe if I just got something to eat, preferably something lemon-flavored if we had it, I'd feel all right and stay asleep.

I tiptoed downstairs and through the dark to the kitchen. Trying to be quiet—I didn't want to explain my intense lemon mania to a soul—I eased open the lighted frig. Dad's Valentine torte, what was left of it, was there. I wished there was a way to turn it into lemon pie, but there wasn't. I was ready to eat a whole lemon if I had to, when I spotted the quart carton of lemon yogurt behind a chunk of leftover ham. Though I was starving for lemon, I'm not that crazy about yogurt. For a minute I didn't know what to do. Then I got a box of chocolate chip cookies from the cupboard. They'd go with the yogurt pretty well, I thought.

I felt like a junkie needing a fix, sitting at the kitchen table shoveling in lemon yogurt, with cookies to make it go down. Two big dishfuls of lemon yogurt and ten chocolate chip cookies later, I stood up, satisfied, my tummy mooned out under my nightgown.

I crawled back into bed, positive that I'd sleep better. I did fall asleep. Then a nightmare hit me in which I was a lemon being twirled to death in a juicer. My own gargling noises woke me, totally out of breath and drizzly with sweat. I was scared to death to go back to sleep, so I barely drowsed from then on. A lot later the alarm went off. I got up but I felt rotten.

Even though I didn't want to go, I dressed for school. I had to face Logan and Lawrie sometime. I had to make up with Rina if she'd let me. But, I decided, if I really had a choice, I would run off to Brazil or somewhere.

Down in the kitchen Mom was in her red robe, making scrambled eggs while Addie and Hans drank their juice at the table. Daddy had already gone, to make sure mail was in the boxes by eight A.M. "Good morning, Calla," Mom chirruped, in her usual morning good mood. She went on cooking, and then, when I didn't say anything, she repeated, "Good morning, Calla."

" 'Morning," I grumbled, sipping my apple juice with my eyes closed.

"My, aren't we a grouch. Have a bad night?"

It's funny how a mother can hit the nail on the head even when she doesn't know what she's talking about.

Addie had her nose in the air. "I smell lemonade. I don't want apple juice. I want lemonade."

"Don't be ridiculous, honey." Mom tossed her hair back and smiled at Addie. "Lemonade is for summertime. You can't smell lemonade."

"It's me," I said.

Mom laughed hard. "I get it. Funnnny. You're admitting you're a sourpuss this morning."

I wasn't, but I couldn't explain. Mom watched me for a minute, and then she came over and kissed me on the forehead. "I know you weren't agreeing that you are a sourpuss. I remember, now, about your science project you started last night. That's why you smell all lemony this morning. Mmm, kind of nice," she sniffed. "Anyway, good luck on the mold, sweetheart. Now, I have to dress for work; Mrs. Lakley is going to be here any second. Have a good day at school."

You don't have a good day at Tarantula City, I wanted to tell her. Instead, I went right on choking down my eggs.

# four

I felt shrivelly inside about school. Really, who cared if I ever got there? Everybody would be pointing and talking about me—why be in a rush to get into that? As I passed the Conser Arms Apartments, I went up and knocked on Mrs. Van Heusen's door, although I had just ten minutes left to get to school.

"Calla Lea!" she exclaimed when she opened the door and saw me. She stood back, her orchid muumuu a tent around her squat form. "Come in, dear. Come in."

Somebody still loved me. "I came to ask if you'll bring flowers for the skit on Saturday." Actually, there was no need to ask. Mrs. V. always brought flowers. I stepped inside and she closed the door. Her house smelled like roses—probably air freshener.

She beamed. "You'll see what I bring on Saturday—they're a surprise! Flowers are hard to come by in mid-winter, you know." For a few minutes we visited. Then, I tried not to think about the time as I stood on a stool, replacing a lightbulb as a favor for her. Later, I sat at her table eating a slice of toast with strawberry jam. The trouble was, Mrs. V.'s kitchen clock was in my line of vision. At three minutes to first bell, I knew I'd better get going, or else.

Everybody was racing toward their classes when I puffed through the door. Rina sailed right by me. "So hang me for being a bubonic-plague-carrying rat!" I whispered to her rigid back, smarting. Rina's aura would turn tears to ice cubes. But I'd expected this from her. I'd give her my best smile anytime I saw her today, I decided. Confuse her. In time she'd get over being mad, maybe, and we would talk.

It amazed me, as I headed toward homeroom, that others paid me no more attention than usual. Then I realized that Logan must not have told anyone he wanted to break up with me. A good sign!

Another good sign was that at least three times during the morning, Logan smiled at me! He didn't stop to talk to me, as he hurried along with his friends between classes, but I couldn't see one iota of difference in the way he smiled at me now and how he'd smiled before the note. The way the rest of the morning passed—there might have been no note, no trouble yesterday. I almost felt as if I'd imagined everything, the lemon episode included.

At lunchtime, I was making for the cafeteria line when I heard a familiar yell: "Hey, Calla, wait for me!" I stopped and looked around, scared I was dreaming for sure. Logan loped toward me, a huge grin on his face. I started to shake, then reminded myself to act natural, not say or do anything that would mess things up. Because Logan appeared truly glad to see me, an answer to my prayers. And maybe lemon power.

"Hi," I said, making room for him in the line. Because I couldn't think of anything else to do, I grabbed a tray and shoved it at him. He took it, that wide slanty grin still on his face, a shine in his green eyes. Something wonderful was going on with him, I could feel it. I hoped it was about me. "Hungry?" I said, still at a loss for sensible conversation, when it used to be that I could talk to him so easily.

Logan's curly head tossed. "Yeah, sure." Then he took a deep breath and looked square at me. "Guess what!"

"What?"

"My dad called last night, and next month I'm going to Texas."

I felt as though someone had hit the back of my

knees from behind. "You're what?" I screeched. Half the people in the lunchroom turned to look at me. I lowered my voice to a shaking whisper. "Y-you're what?"

"I get to go to Amarillo for spring break. Dad called to ask and Mom said I could. And he says he hasn't sold El Cabrillo, yet. I'll get to ride the whole time, Cal!"

I was breathing again. "Oh, Logan, that's good, that's great. I know how much you've missed El Cabrillo, and riding." If Logan was going to Amarillo just for spring break I could handle it. It felt super having him standing beside me again, just like always, his shoulder just a couple inches higher than mine, his elbow brushing my arm. He's mine; Logan Matthew McGee is mine and that's all there is to it, I thought, with a warm flood of returned confidence.

Logan gave me a serious, sideways look. He scuffed his feet and looked the other way. While I waited for him to speak, I was absentmindedly aware that he was not wearing the cowboy boots I was used to seeing on his feet, but ordinary tennis shoes. His Western belt had been exchanged for a regular one, too. When had he started to change and look like the other guys? I made myself pay more attention as he cleared his throat. He was going to say something about the note, I knew it. My own throat went dry as I waited. I clutched my cold, empty tray to my chest, needing something to hang onto.

"Cal..." He looked at me, chewing his lip.

"What?"

"The valentine. The note. I shouldn't have—"

He shouldn't have—Logan was about to apologize, say he'd changed his mind. My heart pumped happily.

He didn't get to finish. Suddenly there was a hoarse boy's laugh, and Logan abruptly disappeared from my vision. "No!" I yelled in protest. What maniac had the nerve to interrupt Logan's beautiful speech to me? I whirled around, feeling murderous, and saw Logan being hauled across the floor, struggling, by Alex Barring-ton, clutching one arm, and Teddy Marks, the other. "Oh, God. Logan, no. Please..." I whispered.

"I guess we're going to Burgerville instead," he called over his shoulder with a shrugging laugh. "They insist. Later, Cal..."

Later. Did he mean the usual "see you around" or did he mean "we'll finish this talk later"? My confused brain swirled as I watched Alex grab Logan's tray from him and sprint back to put it where it belonged. What did he mean? The three of them shuffled through the door, laughing. Two girls waited on the outside. I thought one was Lawrie Stamper, but, not seeing well, I couldn't be sure.

I tried to get myself together. After all, Logan had to be dragged away. It was clear to anybody who might have been watching that he wanted to stay and talk to me. That counted. But still, I hated Teddy and Alex for this. They made me feel unimportant. My eyes burned with tears; then I shook off the bad feeling. I mustn't forget I still mattered to Logan or he wouldn't have wanted to tell me about his trip to Amarillo next month. That was encouraging. More, he'd been about to discuss the valentine and note he'd given me, and retract the note, I was sure. I would see that he got to finish when his stupid friends weren't around!

I lifted my chin and moved forward in the line with the others. Things could be a lot worse.

I filled my plate at the salad bar, got milk and a roll, and took my tray to the nearest table, not bothering to look for Rina and Emmy. Rina probably wouldn't want them to sit with me, anyway, but I didn't much care. A couple of minutes later, Kristin LaSusa and her friends moved in at my table, but after saying hi, that was it with them; they talked and laughed among themselves. Any other time I'd have felt horrible to be by myself, but I was so hopeful about Logan that anything else was okay.

Logan had a meeting to discuss spring track after school, so there was no chance to see him then. Emmy grabbed me for a minute before she caught her bus home. "I'll see you at my program tonight," she said. "And Calla, if Rina snubs you and doesn't want to sit with you, well—don't let it upset you, all right? She likes to act mad, but actually she's getting over it. Wait and see. The three of us are still best friends."

"Sure, Em. Well, I'll see you tonight. Break a leg." I gave her the well-known actor's comment and a thumbs-up for good luck. Em was a friend to keep.

As it turned out, I nearly fell asleep during her performance, having lost so much sleep the night before. I didn't expect Logan to be at the music program, and he wasn't. Although the music kids put on a pretty good show at times, not many people go to the programs besides their close friends and parents. At intermission, I spotted Rina with Lynne Cook. When I walked over to talk, Rina pretended not to see me and ran off giggling with Lynne to the restroom. I could have followed, but I knew Rina wasn't ready to patch things up.

Later, I went home and got into bed. The way Logan had acted today I thought the lemons might be working, so I left them where they were and fell into a heavy sleep.

It would be hard to explain why I went to the senior citizen center every Saturday morning, as I did the next day. I guess I just liked it—liked helping them, liked how they made me feel.

Walking along Harlan Avenue, I remembered that, from the beginning, Emmy and Rina made it plain that they thought I was crazy. I shook my head, smiling to myself, at how they didn't know. Even though her parents were pretty old, Emmy said that old people scared her! Rina said that they smelled bad and most of them were either bossy or crazy.

In my opinion, they were so wrong.

Lots of elderly people who spent their recreational hours at the center were plenty sharp. Many had had interesting careers, and most could tell great stories. Almost all were kind. They were better at raising money for the community than any other group. Making and selling homemade doughnuts was their specialty. At Christmas, hundreds of doughnuts were sold to help the library. Anytime there was a special need in the community, the senior citizens formed a work party and made doughnuts to sell.

They knew how to have fun as well as teenagers did, too. Not just with the once-a-month skits I helped with, but they played bingo, had dances and potluck dinners; or they'd invite in guest musicians or speakers. They took trips, too.

Particularly with my own grandmother gone, I liked going there. It was as if I had inherited lots of neat grandmothers and grandfathers. I wouldn't miss it for anything, except that today I half wished that I was on my way to Logan's house instead, to finish our talk. Tomorrow was Sunday, though, and Logan had always come over to my house on Sundays.

The center was a low building, painted citrus colors outside and in, reminding me of a Sunkist commercial. When I got there, Mabel Van Heusen was waiting inside the main door for me. She exclaimed happily, "Now that you're here, I can tell you about our flowers for the Valentine's Day skit, for the set and all. Pussy willows and forsythia! I scrounged them from neighbors' yards to decorate with, if we need some tall things to look like bushes. And I brought a bowl of my own red camellias, if we need them for an inside scene."

"That's great!" Mrs. Van Heusen, an ace with flowers, kept many friends supplied. She planted the small plots around her apartment by the moon's influence, she'd told me. I smiled as I took off my backpack that held my clipboard. I removed my coat and waited for her to lead the way. Mrs. Shawcross watched us from the "gift shop," a section of the entryway where homemade crafts were sold from behind a counter.

"You're late, aren't you?" Mrs. V said, motioning me to follow. "We're all waiting."

I checked my watch. I was three minutes early.

"Doesn't it make you feel good to be appreciated?" Mrs. Shawcross called to me knowingly from the gift shop. We both knew it was happening again—some of the old people, anxious for me to come, had started watching for me 'way ahead of time. Then, when they had to wait, they thought it must be because I was late. It was kind of funny. I smiled at Mrs. Shawcross.

Mrs. Van Heusen and I joined the others who sat waiting in the main activity room. One old man, whom I knew by his first name, Russell, sat up straighter in his wheelchair when he saw me come in. "She's here!" he barked happily; then he practically cut a wheelie getting over to the television to turn it off. He once had been a race-car driver, somebody'd told me.

"Okay." I grinned around at my attentive group. "Remember last week we decided that you'd think over what you wanted to do about a Valentine's Day skit?

The skit today is to be just for practice. Maybe next summer we can give a real play and charge admission."

"Hearts and flowers," Annie Bybee said.

"Uh, is that a suggestion?" I put down my things and straddled a chair backward, my chin resting on my arms, which crossed on the back.

"She's saying hearts and flowers are connected to Valentine's Day, like pumpkins and black cats on

Halloween," Thelma Merrill rasped. Thelma looked as coarse as her voice sounded sandpapery. But she was kind. Before retirement she'd owned her own drapery business. I thought of one time she'd come to our house, bringing a plate of snickerdoodle cookies. Hans was still a toddler, but a con artist even then. He'd lifted his arms and gurgled and cooed his way onto her lap. Homely Thelma had been so enthralled she'd nearly cried. Naturally, we couldn't tell her that Hans "wanted up" to reach the plate of cookies on the table.

I got my mind back on the subject. "Well, did somebody remember a valentine's experience that we can act out in a skit?"

"We all know what we want to do, love," Mr. Dabler announced, rocking back and forth in his rocking chair, "but I don't know if we can, Calla."

I grinned at him. "Tell me about it and we'll see..." I could always count on dear old Dabler, as Mom called him. Besides being the comic, the friendliest of the bunch, he was also the most helpful. "So what's the idea?"

"It's Annie Bybee's story. Go ahead and tell Calla," he coaxed the bashful little lady across the circle from him.

I looked at Annie Bybee. I'd have bet she'd been the same shy person all of her life, and years hadn't changed her true nature. She lifted her face, framed by snow-white hair, and began softly after a hesitation. "It's about the Valentine's Day in nineteen twenty-seven when my late husband, Charles, proposed. Do you think that will work for our skit, Calla?"

It was a good beginning. "What happened?" I prompted her.

"I'd been thinking to marry this neighbor boy, Emmett Jeffries, you see. Our families had known one another for a long, long time. I was having trouble making up my mind because at the state fair, the summer before, I'd met Charles Bybee. We really had eyes for each other, and I just couldn't get that handsome boy out of my mind."

They all laughed, me with them. A gentleman next to Annie patted her knee.

"Tell Calla what Charlie did." Thelma rasped.

I grinned my thanks for getting Annie back on the subject, when it seemed she'd forgotten.

Annie's smile turned even more youngish and sweet. "Charlie lived in Chicago, a hundred miles away. He couldn't forget me, either, as it turned out," she said. "So the day before Valentine's Day, nineteen twenty-seven, he went out and bought this big red heart box of chocolates. He got on a bus and headed for Little Wood where I lived. Forgot to wear his hat and coat," she laughed, "he was that taken with me."

"And—?" I encouraged her this time.

"Well, it was a cold, windy, rainy day in Chicago.

But Charlie got on that bus and rode a hundred miles to Little Wood. He came to my house the next morning, and Mama asked him to stay for dinner. That's what we called the noon meal in those days—dinner. After dinner we ate Charlie's chocolates, and Mama played songs for us on the piano. Then the folks left us alone, and Charlie and I just talked and talked all that afternoon. Just before sundown, he asked me to marry him."

"Good for him!" Dabler cackled. I silently seconded the motion. This was fun!

"Tell her about the neighbor kid, Emmett, what he did!" Russell called from his wheelchair. He was trying to reach for a glass of water on a table near him. I got up and got it for him, then hurriedly sat down again.

Annie continued, "Well, late that day Emmett, the neighbor boy I'd been going with for three years, he got on his horse and, taking his old sweet time, rode over to my house, bringing me a box of candy, too. 'I'm here to ask for your hand, Annie,' he said. And I told him, 'Well, Emmett, you're a little too late. Charlie By bee just came all the way from Chicago to ask me to marry him and I accepted!' "

Everyone in the room clapped, including me. It was perfect. "It's a good story," I said, laughing. "There's conflict between the characters. And a happy ending. A message, too, that it's a mistake to put something off" too long. I'd like to see us act it out. So what's the problem?" I asked Dabler, since he'd been worried that we couldn't do it.

"What about the bus? I just don't see what we can do about a bus, and her beau's bus ride is important to the story."

"True." I had a couple of skit books in my pack, but I could feel an idea buzzing at the edges of my brain and didn't think I'd need the books for this. "It's the illusion that counts, Mr. Dabler. We don't need an actual bus." I thought about it a few seconds longer. "Look, don't you think a couple rows of chairs can represent the bus? A lot of you can be passengers. More of you can take part in the skit. Okay?"

There was a riffle of happy comments around the room. Dabler clapped his long, bony forehead. "Ain't no trouble with that. We can do it!"

"Chairs in a row like when we were little kids. It'll be fun," somebody else added.

"I thought we gave up stuff like that, but what the hell, I'm game," Russell grunted, grinning.

"Thanks for being a good sport," I told him. Most of the time I felt in control when we were putting on a skit. But then, once in a while, it would hit me how young I was and how much longer the others had lived, how much more they'd seen and knew. I never wanted to put them down in any way, treat them like children, or make them look silly. Mostly I hoped to earn the respect they showed me.

"For Annie's home, all we need is to have the couch center stage, "I said. "We'll put a table with Mabel's camellias next to the couch." Mabel looked proud. I saw her nod and smile at the woman sitting next to her. "That's about all we need for props. Looks easy to me," I told them.

"What about the horse?" Thelma reminded us. "Annie's first beau, Emmett, comes riding up on a horse, remember?"

"Sound effects," I told her. "Sound effects will take care of the horse. One of you can clap your hands against your thighs to make a sound like hoofbeats."

"Like this?" Russell asked. He did a perfect horse imitation on his thin, immobile thighs.

"Great," I nodded. "And, for the opening of the skit when Charlie is getting ready to leave Chicago, we'll drop some rice in an open shoe box, slowly, over and over. That makes a good rain sound."

"Hey, that's a smart idea." Dabler beamed at me.

I smiled at him and made a note about the rice. The center's kitchen should have some. I felt I was getting in good practice plotting and directing skits, and was lucky that the old people here at the center were agreeable, willing to let me lead. Kids my own age would be sassing me or walking off the set if they didn't like something.

Under my direction, everyone who could got busy arranging the set. It got pretty noisy for a while. Mr. Elkins kept saying, "What?!" when he couldn't hear what somebody said, and I'd repeat for him, sometimes more than once, but I didn't mind.

Enough members had turned up, so that, besides performers, we'd have a good audience, which always made the Saturday skits, even the simple ones, more fun.

One of my first times here I'd explained that we didn't need a stage, that we'd have a theater in the round, or arena staging, right here in the center of this big room. Now chairs were moved into two rows downstage center to form the bus.

"Wheelchair people, you don't need to change chairs. Just move into line. Right, you're bus passengers now." I paused. "Mr. Dabler, please put the table and chairs for the living room scene up center stage. That way, when the time comes, the bus passengers can turn their chairs and be audience without a lot of moving around." I was proud of myself for thinking of that. But then, I always felt more capable, more real, more myself, when I was working on a play. It had nothing to do with being grown-up or being a kid—it had to do with doing something I had a feel for and enjoyed, whatever my age.

Later, with the set ready, the others took twenty

minutes for restroom and coffee breaks and just to rest, while I took my clipboard and sketched some quick dialogue and directions. Very improvisational—and definitely not Broadway stuff. But in the time I had, I made it as catchy as I could, to entertain my friends, and complete enough to carry out the story to their satisfaction. I thought it was pretty good.

After that, I lost track of where the next few hours went. They flew by as we picked our cast. Annie Bybee was too shy to play herself and insisted she wanted to "see the action," so we got another lady, Mrs. Edgerman, to play her. Mr. Dabler agreed to be the stage manager and take care of the props. Then we went through a couple of read-throughs, I made some changes, and finally we got into it with the real thing.

Matt Dillon and Richard Gere couldn't have given better performances than some of ours, I thought, watching. Pumped with pride, I felt like the new Lillian Hellman, Gertrude Stein, or somebody.

We got so carried away, having fun, that just about everybody in the room sighed with disappointment when the skit was finally over and there wasn't anything else to do. I got hugged and kissed so much as we were leaving, late in the afternoon, that I almost cried. Not that it was any different from any other Saturday—they made me feel good, and important, every time. It wasn't any wonder I always went back. Sometime, maybe, I would get Rina and Emmy to come and see for themselves what took place.

When I got home, there was a message for me on the corkboard by the phone. Rina had called, it was urgent, and I was supposed to call her back. Rina, huh? I sighed and nodded to myself in relief. She must have finally thawed!

# five

I felt awkward and squeamish about returning Rina's call. What was she going to say? And what should I say to her? I decided to make an onion sandwich while I thought about it.

As I buttered bread in the kitchen, I remembered that Rina had been abandoned by her mother when she was a baby and left to live with just her dad, who owns a big construction business, Treebrook Builders. Before she left, Rina's mother did her a real dirty trick. She named her. Because Rina was born in September, her kooky mom named her after the flower and gemstone of the month. I shook my head and buttered my finger by mistake. Her full name was Asterina Sapphire Reynolds—Rina for short.

I didn't feel too sorry for Rina, though, about her name or anything else. She was good at managing her own affairs and yours, too, if you weren't careful, I reminded myself as I sliced a large onion.

I finished making my sandwich, got a Coke to go with it, and went into the living room. Mrs. Lakley was asleep in Dad's chair. I flipped the TV on. Since the house was quiet, I knew the kids weren't awake from their afternoon naps yet. I was half sorry, because their craziness could sometimes wipe my mind clean of my personal troubles. Then I could begin all new thinking. Unfortunately, I felt very thick-headed, uncertain, and not at all prepared to talk with Rina.

Lakley started making little animal-like sounds as I flipped through the channels with the remote control, but she didn't wake. There wasn't anything on TV that looked interesting. I finished my Coke and sandwich and headed for my room, thinking I could write a few pages of script on my new play. The phone rang.

Even before I could sprint to my room to answer it, I knew it would be Rina calling back.

I took six deep breaths and picked up the phone. "Hello?"

"What are you doing?" Rina asked, her tone as friendly and normal as could be. I wished more than ever that I hadn't called her a hairy orangutan —she wasn't that fuzzy, anyway. Hearing Rina's voice, I realized I had missed her.

"I just got back from the senior citizen center—" I said in a return rush of excitement. I wanted to tell her about my day there, but then I was afraid that Rina might think what we'd done was dull and boring. I didn't want the glad way I felt tarnished by her criticisms. Besides, our friendship was shaky enough; I wouldn't further risk it carrying on about something that wouldn't interest her. Better to butter her up if I could. "I was going to call you. Rina, I'm sorry. I never should have said what I did to you. I didn't mean it. I was just awfully upset that day and—"

"Oh, forget it, Cal. I know you didn't mean what you said," she interrupted. "Anyway, I understand. Now." Her tone was smooth, almost smug, like she had something over on me.

I tried to ignore the prickles of worry. "Then it's okay, we're friends again?" I asked cautiously.

"Sure," she burbled in my ear.

I lay back on my bed, cradling the phone to my ear. Something was up, I was sure. Terror struck my heart. Maybe she'd taken up with Logan to get even with me and now felt she could afford to be nice! "So what's happening, Rina? You and Shiney seeing a movie tonight?"

There was almost a laugh in Rina's voice as she answered my question with a question of her own. "Do you and Logan want to go with us?"

So that was it. She knew! She knew Logan had

dumped me. Or she was guessing he had and wanted to gloat and hurt me back. I'd known Rina a long time, and I could tell when she had something up her sleeve and was baiting somebody. This time it was me. I sat up. "I'm—I'm not s-sure." I felt like a trapped animal and I hated her. But I didn't want to keep fighting. "M-maybe not."

"Because of Kristin LaSusa?" Rina asked innocently.

I felt ill. "Wh-what do you mean?"

"Oh. Oh, maybe I shouldn't have said anything. Shiney and I saw them in the park today, riding around together on their bikes." She paused. "I guess that was while you were at the center with those old people," she finished on an up note, waiting for my response.

And I didn't know what to say. I felt like I'd been suddenly caught under one of those auto smashers at the dump. I could hardly breathe. I'd thought Logan was after Lawrie Stamper—that was bad enough. Now he'd been out riding bikes with still another girl, Kristin LaSusa! Maybe it was Kristin and Lawrie who'd gone off to Burgerville for lunch with the three guys yesterday. No, I remembered, Kristin and her friends had sat at my table at school.

"You there?" There was a shade of sympathy in Rina's voice this time. "Cal, you all right?" It was like asking if I was still alive after being stabbed.

I swallowed hard. "I'm here." I'd thought when Logan started to talk to me yesterday that we were on the verge of getting back together. I was sure of it. I still wanted to hear what he'd been about to tell me.

I knew suddenly that I was going to lie, until I had a chance to talk to him myself and finish our conversation. "Logan and Kris are just friends," I told Rina, glad she couldn't see my face. I scratched my ankle while I tried to think. As a rule, I'm not a great liar. Before this thing with Logan, the last real lie I'd told was when I was six. I had taken all the change from my mother's purse and scattered it all over our front lawn. Then I'd gone out and pretended to suddenly "find" the money. That lie hadn't worked any better than any other I'd ever told, so I'd quit.

I cleared my throat. "They—she sat at my lunch table Friday and said then that Logan—had offered to fix her bike. They were probably at the park just trying out the bike to see if it worked okay." My on-the-spot plot sounded so logical that I wondered if maybe that's what had really happened. It could have been. More confident, I added, "He's coming over either tonight or tomorrow."

"Huh." For several seconds that's all Rina said: "Huh." I didn't know if I'd convinced her that nothing was wrong, that Logan was still my boyfriend. But she went on: "Just so you and Logan haven't broken up. I know how much you guys like each other. And I know how I'd feel. I'd die if Shiney wanted to break up with me."

She must have been only guessing. And surprisingly, in the last few seconds, she'd sounded as though her feelings had changed and maybe she honestly cared. "It would be awful," I said, very quiet. All at once I was dying to tell her the truth—everything. Then I caught myself. It was true that we were talking again, but that didn't mean so much.

Since Logan had dropped me I wasn't sure anymore who was loyal and who was not. I still felt mixed up, confused. "I better go now, Rina. It's almost time for Mom to be home from work, and I haven't made my bed yet or anything." The truth was, I'd let my room go for days now and could hardly find anything I needed in the mess.

"You and Shiney have fun tonight," I said. I didn't mention Logan again. I just hoped he'd come over and unmake me a liar, so I wouldn't feel so awful.

"See you around, Calla."

I thought about our conversation after I hung up and knew that Rina'd wanted to get back at me for the hairy-monkey remark. Well, she had, by reporting that she'd seen Logan with another girl. She'd known how much that would bother me.

Now that she'd told, she considered us even. I knew how Rina thought.

I used to have good insight into most people—or believed I did. I'd wanted to write plays originally because I felt I knew what made people tick, and it would be fun to create my own characters and bring them to life in scenes and such. I didn't feel so sure about knowing people anymore.

Like Logan. How or why he got the idea to break up with me I couldn't fathom. We had hardly fought at all. And I thought we'd had a lot of fun. Maybe I was too dull for him since I didn't drink beer or smoke pot. But Logan didn't, either; none of my friends did. I didn't know about Kristin LaSusa, but I thought Lawrie Stamper might, at parties anyway. I couldn't say for sure because my friends and I never got invited to those kinds of parties.

I had to talk to Logan and that's all there was to it. After I got off the phone with Rina, I tried to work on my play. It's about this teenage girl who is so afraid of making mistakes that that is all she does, blunder around making one mistake after another from trying to be too careful. There was a girl like that in seventh grade. I felt it was going to be a comedy. But this time I couldn't keep my mind on it.

Finally, I gave up on the scene, deciding that tomorrow, Sunday, might be a better time to work on it if Logan didn't come around, if he came by tonight instead.

Since it was Saturday night, Dad took the whole family to supper at Taco John's, which we love. We weren't gone long. After we returned I waited in my room for Logan to ring our doorbell or call on the phone. When he hadn't by bedtime, I told myself stubbornly that he would tomorrow. From the time I met him, Logan had always come to see me on Sundays.

Next day I showered and shampooed my hair, early. Instead of just combing my short bangs into place, I used the curling iron, fluting them back. I brushed all of my hair up one side and over and braided it in a single braid to hang over one shoulder; I tied it with a strand of white lace. Then I thought about digging into my old sweaters for one that was too tight, but when I pictured my bust compared to Lawrie Stamper's, I threw that idea out. You don't fight melons with fried eggs. I settled for a clean white shirt and jeans and a pair of drop earrings an inch long.

"You sure look cute this morning, Calla," Mom said when I came down to breakfast.

"Thanks, Mom." I twirled around, gave my bangs a flick, and grinned. I then heaved a deep sigh, determined that this was going to be a better day than those I'd been having lately. I liked it in the kitchen, with the little kids chattering cozily at the table with Dad, instead of fighting, and good smells coming from the breakfast Mom was making.

" 'Morning, Bright Eyes!" Dad pulled me onto his knee for a hug. When Addie looked mad, he pulled her onto the other knee and then piled a laughing Hans on top of us. "Look at my crew, Valerie," he said to Mom. "Best-looking kids in the whole world and I just love 'em." I felt embarrassed, I was hardly a little kid anymore, but I didn't want to hurt Dad's feelings. I laughed along with the little kids for a minute and kissed Dad's forehead where the hair is starting to get a little thin. Then I stood up and rearranged the kids.

"Get your good-looking crew over here for breakfast and stop bragging," Mom said with a scorn she plainly didn't mean. She got the butter and syrup from the frig, humming, and closed the door with her backside. I moved to help her. She smiled, a nice, special smile she has for me sometimes, like she's thinking, Hey, there's my almost grown daughter, my equal, my friend. "Will you get the French toast from the microwave, please, Cal?"

All at once I got a tight pain in my throat. I wanted to talk to her about everything that'd happened the past few days and ask her advice. But I didn't think I could, even if the time had been right, which it wasn't. And, I thought, swallowing the knot, I might not need to talk to her if Logan came today and we straightened things out. With a pair of mitts I carried the hot platter of fluffy toast to the table.

If he came, I wanted to do something Logan liked, I thought as I ate breakfast. The mall was dead on Sunday, but maybe we could shoot baskets at his place like we had lots of times. Or we could go biking at the park, like he'd done yesterday with Kristin. If he'd kissed her at the park—but I couldn't think about that. I breathed deep to get rid of my feeling of suffocation and took a quick shot of orange juice.

I knew there was a riding stable outside town where Logan went sometimes when he was really missing his dad and Texas badly. I didn't know how to ride a horse, but maybe it was time we went out there so Logan could teach me. I decided that that idea was the best of the bunch. I'd ask Dad to drive us there as soon as Logan showed up. My mind was made up.

"Pass more o.j., please!" I told Dad.

"Need your nourishment for a big day, huh?"

I nodded. "You bet." I didn't want to look ridiculous if Logan didn't come, so I didn't say anything more right then. But, of course, he would come. "When are we going to get a VCR?" I blurted. "Everybody's family at school has one—" As I'd known it would, that led to a lengthy discussion of how the federal government hadn't seen fit to raise

Dad's salary in a "blue moon," how we actually lived a pretty good life as it was, and doing without some things built character, anyway, et cetera, et cetera.

It was my own fault that I had to sit through the whole discussion. After I helped Mom clear the breakfast dishes, I started a chocolate cake for dinner, while Mom and Dad read the Sunday papers in the living room. All the time that I measured and mixed I listened for the doorbell or an extra voice from the living room— Logan's.

While the cake baked I sat on the living room floor with Addie and Hans and helped with their puzzle. I couldn't help looking at the silent door every once in a while.

Later, I colored a picture for the kids with my pastels. While I colored, Hans and Addie bounced and carried on like I was performing some kind of glorious magic. I take art and I'm good but not that good. Tears burned my eyes, but I wasn't sure if it was because of the shrimps thinking I was great, or that Logan hadn't come. Yet.

A couple times I said I had to go to the bathroom and then went upstairs to stand awhile at the front window where I could see down Conser Street several blocks. The whole street stayed empty and gloomy with drizzling rain. I thought of the cheerful morning that I'd thought was an omen for a happy day, and a hard knot formed in my throat.

Time dragged. I helped the kids pick up their toys, and then we found an ancient Tarzan movie on TV. Dad gave up an NBA basketball game to watch, too. He said he'd seen the movie the first time when he was about seven. It was disgusting how excited he got, watching it now. Anybody could see that it was a stupid movie. I was restless all through it. I wished I had something else to do, but I didn't say so out loud.

After lunch, Mom and the kids disappeared for naps. Dad went into the study to plink around on the computer. We do own a computer, because Dad says it is a lot more practical and useful than a VCR. Since the first of January, he'd been trying to program a budget, or something. Me, I don't know a byte from a buffer, but next year in high school I'll study computers, because that's the way the world is going. I wouldn't mind writing plays on a word processor.

In my room, which I hadn't felt like cleaning yesterday, after all, I dumped rumpled clothes off my desk onto the floor and got out my comedy script. I tried to imagine a scene where my lead character was supposed to loan a friend a dance dress. Only she gives her the wrong box. And just before the big affair, the friend opens the box and finds a dried floral spray from another character's funeral. When I'd planned the scene two weeks before, I'd laughed at the idea until I'd cried. Now, trying to put it into catchy dialogue, it was definitely morbid and dumb.

It was useless to try to be funny when my mood was anything but. I abandoned the scene on my desk and threw myself on the rumpled bed. I lay there for a long time, trancelike, just waiting. Waiting. Logan would come. There was still time.

It was six o'clock by my bedside clock radio when Mom called everybody downstairs to eat seconds on cake. The day had been the longest and most boring of my life. Whatever good feelings I'd had in the morning were long gone. Downstairs, with a feeling of bitter disgust, I watched Addie and Hans, energized by their naps, behave like animals —yammering with their mouths full, goofing off, and getting cake from their ears to their knees. A cake I had worked hard on. When I couldn't take it anymore, I asked Mom, "Why don't you make them behave?"

She gave me a funny look. "I suppose, because they aren't having the same effect on me that they evidently are having on you. But when they do need scolding, Dad or I will take care of it."

"Well, they make me sick," I snapped.

"Whoa, babe. Aren't you getting a little carried away?" Dad looked at me in surprise. "Get down off your high horse, Bright Eyes. Speaking of horses," he changed his voice to a mock Western drawl, "where's your fella today? I ain't seen him around the last few days. You suppose he went and got himself another gal?"

I jumped up from my chair, feeling like a bomb whose fuse had finally been lit. "Shut up! Just shut up!" I hissed. I felt horror at seeing my father's shocked expression, but was too confused and angry to back down.

"Calla, my goodness—" Mom began. "Sit down. Apologize to your father—"

"No." Something inside me cracked, but I had to say it.

"What?" Mom looked like I had hit her.

I glared back at her, about to choke. "I said no." I turned and ran for the living room. I had to get out, away from their dumb, open-mouthed faces. Even Addie and Hans were quiet, and Hans looked ready to cry.

"Calla, come back here," Dad ordered.

"Don't tell me what to do!" I snarled over my shoulder. "I'm going for a walk."

As I whipped my coat from the hall closet I heard Mom say, "What on earth has gotten into her? What happened today, anyway?"

"Tell me," Dad said. "I thought we were having a nice, quiet Sunday till a second ago." I could hear the disbelief, the puzzlement, in his voice. "For God's sake, I hope it's temporary and that for some reason she just needs to let off steam. That Texas kid didn't come by today, but I can't see why—" I slammed the door, putting an end to their voices.

Outside, it was starting to get dark. Cold raindrops mixed with the warm tears on my face. My throat hurt so badly that I could hardly swallow. I couldn't think where to go. Emmy lived too far out in the country to go there. I wasn't ready for Rina's yet. I'd just walk, I decided, and be by myself.

I ended up running, running the four blocks west to the new part of town where Logan lived. In a few minutes, I stood across the street from the white duplex where he lived with his mom. I began to shiver and laugh at the same time. There were no lights on in their apartment. Trinket's yellow convertible was not in their carport. The Sunday paper was still in their box. Logan and his mom had gone somewhere for the day, leaving very early, and they still weren't home. That's why he hadn't come over.

The rain beat down on me as I turned back toward home, but I didn't care. I raised my chin and let the sting of it sluice my fears, all my confused emotions, away. I wanted to shout my relief, my happiness, to the world.

Tomorrow, Monday, I'd be back in school and I'd corner Logan. We'd talk, and talk, and talk. And everything would be okay.

# six

The next day I planted myself at the school entrance. I scrunched back under the overhang, but cold rain still blew in on me. I watched the whole school pass by. Some kids looked at me like I was crazy for standing there, but nobody said anything other than hi.

I'd arrived right after the janitors opened up, so I knew Logan hadn't come yet. Finally, I looked out and saw him rushing up the walk, hands jammed into his jacket pockets, his hair plastered into cute little ringlets like he'd just gotten out of the shower. For the second time, I realized he was dressing like everybody else now, not Western. "Hi!" I moved out into the rain in front of him as he came up the steps. Logan looked as surprised as if I'd said, "This is a holdup."

"We have to talk," I explained.

He shook himself like a puppy and hand-brushed the excess rain from his hair before he said, "It's raining."

"Like cats and dogs," I nodded.

"So do we have to stand here? Can't we get out of it?"

I laughed, embarrassed, and moved. "Sorry. Sure, we can talk inside. Where do you want to go? The library?"

It used to be that Logan grabbed my hand as soon as he saw me and we'd walk into school that way. Now, not only did he not take my hand, he acted as if he had something else he ought to be doing. Something more fascinating than getting in out of the rain with me. He frowned a little, but he said, "Okay."

I led the way down the hall to the library. Miss Otto, the librarian, with her huge hairdo settled on her shoulders like a lion's mane, guarded the room from her desk by the door. With a look, I asked Logan to follow me to a far corner where I pretended to examine a shelf of books on world history.

"What's on your mind?" he said to my back. I'd been all ready to ask if he still liked me, if the note had been a mistake like he'd indicated on Friday, if he wanted to go with me again like before. I'd been ready to swear off sweet onion sandwiches if he had a problem with that. But when I turned to look at him, my heart started hammering wildly, it seemed to climb into my throat, my tongue froze...

I stared at Logan. The bell would ring any second and we'd have to go to class. Why couldn't I say something, now that I had the chance?

Relief filled his face the longer I said nothing; then Logan shrugged. "It's been great seeing you, Calla," he said finally, starting away with a jaunty swing. "If that's all..."

"Logan—" I croaked.

He turned back, talking fast. "I think it's neat how you're taking our breaking up, not being mad or crying or anything. The guys say some girls get crazy and give them a rotten time. But I knew you wouldn't be like that." He smiled nervously and again tried to get away.

Wouldn't I be? "Wait, wait a minute," I protested, my throat dry. "Wh-where did you go yesterday?"

He looked put off but answered, "Sun-Corn gave Mom some free tickets to a fancy restaurant in Portland. We spent the day, toured an old mansion, went to the Oregon Museum of Science and Industry, and stuff."

"I wondered why you didn't come over." I tried not to whine, but my voice was hollow, odd even to me.

A quizzical frown grew on his face. "Come over?" Then he said pointedly, "Janni Myers went with Mom and me."

A third girl? Already? It had only been a few days. He liked still another girl? My mind spun. He didn't keep one girl long enough for me to attack her, even! I protested, "B-but Friday, you started to say s-something about the valentine you gave me, and the note. R-re-member, we were in the lunch line to-together."

"Oh, yeah," he looked sheepish. "I sort of had second thoughts—"

In spite of everything, my heart leaped. "Second thoughts?"

He nodded. "I realized I shouldn't have stuck the note about wanting to break up in with the valentine. I should have given them to you separate."

I felt like I was shrinking down into a little ball of nothing. That's what it was? That's what he'd been about to tell me? And all the time I'd thought —All he'd wanted to say was that he should have given me the note separate from the valentine! I tasted something bitter. He'd never meant to say it was all a mistake and he wanted us to be together. Like from another world, the bell chimed and out in the hall the sounds of shuffling feet picked up tempo.

"Gotta go!" Logan said brightly, waving as he hurried off.

I watched him go, reminding me for all the world of a fish, off the hook, swimming happily out of my reach. Logan was really not mine anymore?

"Somebody's crazy!" I yelled, forgetting where I was.

Miss Otto leaped to her feet. "What did you say?"

"N-n-nothing. I—I just thought it was odd that Europe has—so many more people than the US does. Per square mile, I mean."

She eyed me suspiciously, although she sat back down and picked up the pencil she'd dropped. I thought the explanation for my scream was pretty good, considering how fast I'd had to come up with it, but I was sweating.

"Don't you have a classroom to go to?" she asked, carefully calm now. "It's after bell, you know."

"After bell," I nodded, hedging toward the door, "I didn't realize; I'd better hurry." I slid past her puzzled look, and out into the hallway.

I was the last one to homeroom. But luckily, the teacher, Michael Grimes, was still calling roll, and he hadn't yet reached the 5 's. I slipped into my seat while his head was down looking at his roll sheet. I caught Emmy smiling worriedly at me from across the way. When I found Rina at her place three desks behind me, she smiled sympathetically, too. I could sense Logan at his desk over by the windows, but I couldn't look in that direction for anything.

Rina and Emmy stared at me all through first period. Like they thought I'd burst out crying or possibly even fall into a coma at my desk right before their eyes. And the truth was, I felt like doing both, crying first and then fainting so I wouldn't have to feel anything. I guessed the word was definitely out that Logan had dumped me. Maybe he'd made an announcement to that effect over the intercom after he'd left me in the library, and I'd missed it, I decided in a nasty humor. Suddenly fighting mad, I smiled big at Emmy, then Rina, like nobody in the world was happier than me. Maybe to Logan I was dog meat, but I still wasn't going to show I'd been trampled on.

For the rest of the day I felt wretchedly sick, the worst I'd ever felt in my life. But on the outside I made like a clown, the life of the party, a joker. I should have gotten Broadway's Tony Award. I laughed so hard at nerdy Deanie Jones's stupid jokes at lunchtime that he thought I was flirting with him. He trapped me at my locker just before English lit and told me he liked me—really liked me, if I knew what he meant. Unfortunately I did. I told him as nicely as I could, winning a second Tony for Best Actress in a Crisis, that I liked him, too. But that I wanted to be "single" for a while and not go with anybody.

During literature class I got called on to read aloud. Normally, with my flair for drama, I'm the best reader in the room. But when I looked up from my book, I caught Logan flirting with Lawrie

Stamper, giving her that look, his eyelids at half-mast and a smirk on his face. Her again, with a look on her face like a cat that got the cream. When I saw him wink at her and pass her a note, I choked up. I read terribly, lost my place, stuttered, and stammered. The whole class acted antsy and bored, and I thought it would never end.

It was a miracle to me when the three-o'clock bell rang that I had survived the day. I felt like I'd faked my way through a holocaust.

I walked out the school door feeling blind, my whole body numb. Emmy must have caught the country bus home; Rina must have taken off somewhere with Shiney Malone, I thought vacantly. Whatever, I was alone, going nowhere.

A couple of tears rolled down my face as I walked. I'd lost Logan. It was for sure and, somehow, I had to get used to the idea.

I had to get away, be alone for a while, not be at school or home or at a friend's. Colburn's mall was the answer, even though going there after school without permission was strictly forbidden. I was supposed to relieve the babysitter, Mrs. Lakley, as soon as I could get home from school. Worse, I was on probation because I had flipped out and yelled at my parents on Sunday. For double reasons I was supposed to go straight home.

I knew I was putting my head in a sling when I headed down South Harlan Avenue for the mall, but I didn't care. I had to go where it was cheery, where I could be around people who didn't know me, where I could just wander and think and not be bothered.

The windows of most of the mall shops were decorated with colorful fake daffodils, tulips, and hyacinths. Spring? I moved into the flow of people walking the bright corridors and tried not to think about Logan—or about how much trouble I was going to be in at home. Instead, I tried to put my mind on spring, on better things coming, like swimming at the beach, camping, and the downtown summer theater where sometimes they let me help out.

The problem is, when you love someone as much as I loved Logan, your emotions are going to carry on however they want. I couldn't get him out of my mind, I couldn't stop hurting, I couldn't help wanting him back. My first thought in the morning and my last at night had always been the same: Logan. That wouldn't ever change.

I must have wandered around for forty-five minutes or more when it hit me that I was totally starved. But that was my penalty for laughing at Deanie Jones's dumb jokes all noon hour instead of eating lunch. I found a bakery and was about to order a raspberry crown when I saw their Texas-sized doughnuts. That made me think of Logan right off again, and tears shot to my eyes. I told the clerk I'd changed my mind and went on. Later, I bought nachos. They reminded me of Logan, too, since his mom had come to Treebrook to work as a secretary in the Sun-Corn tortilla chip factory, which probably produced these same corn chips under the cheese sauce. But by now I was so starved that I got the nachos down.

The nachos didn't taste as good as usual because of my low mood, but they filled my stomach. When I'd finished them, I threw the paper tray in a waste-basket and went into a big, ritzy department store that Dad says specializes in keeping husbands on the brink of poverty. But it was Dad who'd bought Mom a blue silk blouse here once, which she took back, saying the blouse was too expensive and she'd never feel comfortable in it.

I stopped at a cosmetics counter to look for a freebie sample to dab on my wrist. I was sniffing my perfumed arm when I caught sight of my reflection in the mirror. I stopped sniffing and stared. My pale, drab face was about as pretty as a pancake—I looked pukey! No wonder a cute guy like Logan had lost interest and was looking at all the other girls. What had happened to me? Was I worrying about other stuff so much that I'd forgotten my looks, except for yesterday, which he'd missed.

I started away in a daze. I didn't know what I could do, except go home and dive into my makeup box and do something. So at first, as I stumbled by, I didn't pay much attention to the sign on the corner of the glass counter. Then I went back and read it again: SPRING MAKEOVER SPECIAL—FREE FROM LESLEY MODE.

I looked around. There was a beautiful auburn-haired clerk in a green lab coat beginning to make up an older woman who sat on a stool by the counter. I circled them for a few minutes, like a bloodhound on the scent. The beauty specialist first would get a dab of something from a jar or tube. Then she would spread and pat it onto the woman's face, which, without the makeup, had been about as attractive as a toad's backside. Then, with color sticks of this and that, she began to form the most gorgeous features on the lady. If I hadn't seen the miracle taking place with my own eyes, I wouldn't have believed it.

I wondered if the beauty expert, cosmetologist, or whatever she was called, could make me as beautiful as, say, Susan Lucci on the soap "All My Children." I thought she could. I was watching her create a fantasy from almost nothing.

It was obvious to me now, there had been a change in Logan's feelings for me. But maybe it was only a mere lapse, and his feelings could be heated up again if I got so gorgeous I knocked his socks off. I moved closer to see the action better.

The cosmetologist looked at me with gorgeous, big blue eyes and smiled. "Are you interested in a makeover?"

Was I! I said nervously, "Yeah, yeah, I think I am."

She nodded. "I'll get you another beauty expert. Ann," she called to a clerk who was placing bottles of nail polish in a glass display case, an aisle over from us. "This young lady would like a makeover."

I gulped as Ann, a small, pretty brunette, came toward me. She looked surprised, I guess, at my age or maybe at my dilapidated state. But she smiled, put on her green lab coat, and murmured something like, "Oh, well." She motioned me onto a second stool. "First time?" she asked as she tied the ribbons of a pink cape at the back of my neck.

I told her it was and added that I knew about makeovers and had wanted one for a long time.

Ann, who smelled wonderful, explained that she would begin by "preparing my skin" with cleansers and stuff. Later, she said, we would discuss the colors I liked to wear, so the makeup could be coordinated. I began to feel really excited as she set out bottles and trays of things on the counter. She started swabbing my face with something wet and deliciously perfumy.

My beauty expert was explaining the tools and

makeup she was using as she smeared my face with something and then began to dab at my eyelids. But I was too excited to hear what she was saying. I kept thinking how Logan was going to react when he saw me for the first time with my new look.

In a few minutes, she held up a mirror so I could see what was happening so far. I sucked in my breath and stared. I didn't want to stop looking at myself. She wasn't even done with me—only one eye was finished—but it was smoky and smudgy and sexy! I looked nineteen at least.

Logan's eyes were going to pop out! After this change, he'd never want anyone but me. There wasn't another girl in Treebrook Middle School who'd come close.

I sat back to let Ann do her thing. I was intensely glad I'd skipped going home to come to the mall. No matter what punishment Mom and Dad lined up for me, I knew it would be worth it.

# seven

On the stool a few feet from me, the other woman was finished. A now-glamorous face looked out from the deep blond waves of her hair. I was so fascinated by the difference in her, I couldn't take my eyes away to check my own progress or listen to my own beauty expert as she explained something about "the right makeup brush for the right job." I had every confidence that this was going to work out wonderfully, anyway.

The other woman's cosmetician ducked out of sight behind the counter. Her hand came up to place small, different-shaped boxes, one after another, on the glass countertop above her head. Two dozen pretty boxes in flowered pale green, minimum. The newly made-up woman opened her purse and took out her checkbook. Checkbook? The makeover was supposed to be free!

I realized then that she was buying makeup to take home, not paying for what they'd used to turn her into someone who looked like Ginger Rogers. Did they expect you to buy when they offered a free makeover? I realized in panic that I hadn't thought ahead to anything more than using the tricks I'd learned, with the makeup stuff I had at home.

The blonde older lady stood like a professional model now, watching her purchases being totaled. "Two hundred and thirty-six dollars," the cosmetician told her with a smile.

I nearly fell off my stool. In my own wallet, after buying the nachos, was about forty-eight cents! I had to get out of this! And I'd better explain my situation before my expert, Ann, put in any more time and effort on me. I racked my brain for an explanation that wouldn't sound like it was coming from a dumb, crazy kid. I considered: "I'm trying several makeovers today before I decide to buy." Or: "I'm going to wear Lesley Mode makeup home today, and if it doesn't give me a rash, I'll be back tomorrow." Fair.

The phone by the cash register buzzed; the auburn-haired beauty expert caught it. She looked our way. "Ann, it's for you. Greg," she said with a knowing smile, holding out the receiver. I couldn't believe my luck as Ann happily abandoned me to talk to Greg, a boyfriend, from the look on her face.

As soon as the redhead turned away, too, I slipped off the stool, snatched off the cape, and left the cosmetics department, jamming my arms into my jacket as I went. I darted to the next department, lingerie, and ducked into a forest of silky nightgowns and robes. I stayed there awhile, pretending to be shopping, too scared to peek out and see if they were looking for me back in cosmetics. Grandma used to call her moisturizer "vanishing cream," I remembered, giggling silently, because it was supposed to get rid of her wrinkles. Across the way, did they think they'd used too much of such stuff" on me, wiping me into oblivion?

I would do something with that, in a play some time, I thought with satisfaction.

In a while, it was evident that my getaway had been clean; I could leave. For all I knew, Ann was still on the phone with Greg and was glad I'd departed.

As I headed for the main door, I saw a bra on a mannequin. I stared at the gorgeously curved bust, the beautiful bra, and then I went over to the counter to look for the same bra among the stock. Not that I had the money for it, but I wanted to examine it for future reference. I found it, but in my size it was a scrap of nothing. I picked up another one that looked more the size I wished I was—a size D underwire, by the tag. I wondered what the word "décolleté" meant? If I had enough of me to put into such a bra, I could sure put Lawrie Stamper to shame. But it was useless.

With a sigh, I put the bra down. At the same time, I caught sight of my reflection in the mirrored post off to my left. One eye looked large and bruised, the other small and natural. One cheek was covered with so much blush I looked like I had a fever. The other side of my face—undone—by comparison looked dead and ready for burial.

I started to scream and then put a hand over my mouth because of where I was. I looked like Halloween. I looked worse than that! I had to get to a restroom and wash my face. Maybe if the beauty expert could have finished, I'd be beautiful by now. As it was, I looked like a ghoul. I took a few swift turns, trying to remember which floor the restrooms were on, remembered that they were on this floor, over by the shoes, and sped in that direction. There was a sudden flurry of sound behind me and a hand clamped on my arm. I jerked and looked into the angry eyes of a gray-haired clerk.

"What do you think you're doing?" she demanded.

What I was doing was heading for a restroom to wash my face, but somehow I knew that wasn't what she meant. "N-nothing," I stammered. "Going —restroom," I got out through a fear-tightened throat. I tried to smile. "I-I'd better go—"

"Oh, no, you're not." She stood erect and looked swiftly around. "You're waiting right here for the store detective. I've already rung for him."

I almost stopped breathing. A detective, why a detective? I could see a man in a dark business suit coming our way, and I started to shake. Tears scalded my eyes. "I didn't do anything," I protested in a weak voice. I couldn't believe they were going to arrest me for trying to leave with half of a free makeup job, but it looked like that's what was going to happen.

"What's the problem here?" The detective approached us, rubbing his forehead with his thumb. "Shall we go to my office and talk about it?"

"I didn't do anything," I blurted, "honest, I didn't. The sign said the Lesley Mode makeover was free, and--"

"What?" He stared at me.

The clerk interrupted, "She was stealing a bra!"

My mouth dropped open and I whimpered in protest, shaking my head. "That isn't so! I was looking at the bras, but I didn't try to take one."

"Then what do you call that?" The clerk pointed at the front of me. I looked down, shocked to see the size D underwire décolleté bra hanging between my jeans' legs, the strap caught over a button of my jacket. "I didn't know it was there," I said faintly. "I really didn't. I thought I put it back in the bin, I meant to, but maybe I missed. Or it caught on my button as I turned to leave—"

The store detective was trying not to grin. I hoped, I prayed, that he believed me. But the gray-haired clerk still behaved like a hawk who wanted to peck my eyes out. She snorted, "It's a good story, but I think you were trying to make it look like an accident. Then, as soon as you could turn around where I couldn't see you, you were going to hide the bra on your person."

She was totally wrong.

The detective looked me over carefully. I saw doubt in his face—I hoped it was doubt about my being guilty—but I couldn't tell for sure. Visions of going to jail—and, worse than that, having to have my parents bail me out—eased up a bit. He appeared to like me. "You can go," he nodded. I felt like hugging him.

"Sir, I truly believe I caught this girl in the act of theft. She was stealing this bra." The clerk waved the big D.

"What would she do with it?" the detective queried. I got hot in the face and looked quickly to see if he was looking at my body again. He wasn't. He was studying the clerk as though he wondered if she had soup for brains.

"I wouldn't have any use for the bra," I agreed,

feeling suddenly brave again. I went on to explain to the unsmiling clerk the whole story about the free makeover and leaving and looking this way because I didn't have the money to buy any of the products the beauty expert was showing me.

"That's silly. Everyone knows there is no obligation to buy when you get a free makeover," she sniffed.

"I didn't know it," I protested. "May I leave now, to wash my face?" I wasn't asking her, I was asking the detective. He nodded and motioned for me to go ahead. "Thank you," I said around the lump in my throat. I hated being thought of as a criminal. As I walked away I could hear the detective gently arguing down the clerk's persistent belief that I was a thief.

As I cleaned my face in the restroom, I realized why I was so tempted to go back and kick her shins, and remind her that the bra was out in plain sight, obviously caught on my button by accident. It wasn't the clerk, foolish though she was, that I was really mad at, though—it was me. Because I'd done wrong in coming here in the first place. Even without jail, I was still in hot water and I'd brought every bit of it on myself.

As I was leaving the mall, far down the corridor to my left I saw an old man, waving his hat. It was Mr. Dabler, and he was waving at me. I hesitated when I saw what looked like spilled packages at his feet. Just then I saw two women converge on him from the open doorway of a store. They stooped and began gathering his things. I was glad, because I really needed to get home.

I was frantic with worry all the way home: If I admitted I'd gone to the mall, would I be punished less than if I lied and was later found out? I didn't want to do it, but I felt I had no choice but to lie. It was a terrific risk, but Mom and Dad might never know the difference. There was a chance I'd get off free and everything would be okay, provided I could then live with my conscience. I'd discovered, back when I was little, that a big lie only complicated things and that you almost always wished you could take it back. I was nervous, but I tried not to think about that.

Dad was reading the paper and Mom was on the phone when I got there. "So—you didn't see her at all after school? Thank you, Rina." Mom spoke calmly into the telephone, but from her expression I could tell she was on the edge of being frantic.

"Mom?"

She whirled to look at me from the telephone bench. "Calla! Where have you been? Are you all right?" Her voice was as frazzled as her appearance.

I nodded nonchalantly and tossed my backpack on the sofa. Sucking in my breath and keeping my eyes on her chin so she couldn't read me, I said, "I tried to call Lakley to tell her I had to stay after school. But the line was busy. I had three makeup drawings to do in art and they wouldn't let me go. Sorry, Mom." I sagged onto the couch and leaned back. "God, I'm hungry."

"You should be—you missed dinner," Dad spoke up. His newspaper crackled. "I can't believe schools these days, causing kids to miss their meals."

Mom nodded, her look shrewd. "Are you sure you were kept in? It's after six, Calla. They kept you for more than three hours? And they didn't call me?"

"No," I said, after a hesitation, "that's not how it happened." I picked at a loose upholstery thread next to my thigh. "The art teacher left, forgot I was there, I guess. What happened was that—I got locked inside the school—by accident. The janitor went to his pickup for something he needed and to have a cigarette. It was a long time before he came back and—and found me waiting inside—by the front door." I held my breath; Mom still didn't look convinced.

She sighed. "I want to believe you, Calla, so why am I having trouble?"

I didn't know. Except that my inventive mind might not be doing its best under such terrific pressure. And maybe my face said "lie"; it sure felt neon warm.

Dad spoke up. "Val, you know Calla always tells us the truth."

"Yes, as a rule she does. I'm sorry for the third degree, Callie, but I've been so worried. And poor Mrs. Lakley missed her quilting meeting where she was supposed to give a presentation on historic patterns." She looked at Dad. "Do you think we should talk to the principal?"

"Why?" I lunged forward. Terrified that I'd given myself away, I sat back and attempted a calm, straight face.

"Because—he needs to know that the art teacher was lax and forgot all about you," Mom explained. "And he should be told that the janitor was loafing on the job."

"Mom, they're only human!"

Dad rattled his paper again. "Forget it, Val. It was an honest mistake. No harm done."

"I suppose." She stood up and smiled at me. "It must have been scary for you for a while, locked in that way? C'mon, sweetheart, I've kept your chicken and rice hot for you." When I got up, she put her arm around my shoulders and walked me to the kitchen. Something in her behavior was as phony as the lie I'd told. Was she onto me?

Dinner stuck in my throat and I went up to my room early. There was a gross lemon smell in the room. A week had passed, no wonder! I lifted my pillow, snatched up the crinkled, bluish globs, and threw them in my already overflowing wastebasket. I looked around in disgust from the edge of the bed, wondering how I'd come to this. I hadn't changed the bedsheets; I didn't keep up my room at all. I used to. Instead, I was doing something stupid right and left. The lemons, the makeup deal—lying. I felt turned wrong side out. I hardly knew myself. It seemed that from the time I'd gotten Logan's note on Valentine's Day, an alien had moved into my body.

Before Logan, I'd been a perfectly normal, sane person. If a prize had been offered for a nice, normal, all-around kid, I'd have won it. But I was happy, then. My life wasn't complicated like now. I wondered if falling in love with somebody always makes you crazy and has so much misery connected with it?

After a while, a thought occurred to me that I'd never dreamed I'd have: I wished I'd never met Logan McGee. And if I couldn't have him, if he was going to be the "lover darling" of every girl in Treebrook Middle School, then he could rot in hell, for all I cared!

Suddenly, furiously, I wanted him out of my mind, out of my heart, out of my room. I raced around and gathered up everything he'd given me—stuffed animals, cologne, bracelet, notes, all of it—and piled it on the bed. It was too much for my wastebasket, so I went downstairs and came back with an ugly black plastic garbage bag that suited perfectly. With everything jammed inside, I ran downstairs and out to the back porch and shoved it into the trash can, then took a long, deep breath. It was done. Finished. Logan was no more.

I felt a lot better, back upstairs, lying on my bed. For perhaps ten or fifteen minutes, I felt fine. Then, feeling like I'd discarded a portion of my soul, I knew I couldn't do it. I ran back downstairs and got the bag back from the trash.

Mom was in the kitchen getting a drink of water when I came through. "Calla, what now?" she asked, staring at the garbage bag that I was bringing in instead of taking out.

One more weird thing in a whole string of weirds, I told myself. But to her I said, attempting a smile, "I threw away some stuff I've now decided to keep in a carton on my closet shelf. Stuff that means more to me than I realized, but that I don't want out where I'd have to look at it all the time." The truth.

Mom shook her head. "Calla Lea Stafford, you never cease to amaze me."

"Me, too," I admitted over my pain. "I never cease to amaze me, either, Mom." That was true, too. I didn't know what was going to happen to me, and it scared me.

When I was little, a slimy kid once told me that he bit the heads off sparrows. I was so full of hate and unhappiness when I got up the next morning, I could have. Easily.

Maybe Mom had a clue to what had been in my garbage bag the evening before, and what was going on, or maybe she didn't. But as she slopped oatmeal into my bowl at breakfast, she asked blithely, "What's Logan doing these days, Cal? Haven't seen him around. It used to be he was underfoot all the time."

"Why aren't there raisins in the oatmeal, or dates or something?" I screamed, ignoring her question. "Nobody can eat this puke." God, I hated for her to stick her nose in my business. I would tell her that Logan was no longer my boyfriend when I was ready. She had no right to push.

Like I'd really wanted to know, Mom started coolly explaining about the plain oatmeal: "Because Addie Marie hasn't been able to stomach raisins since their imitation tobacco chewing stunt, and you know Hans hates dates."

"Yeah, but what about me? You never consider what I like. Should I have to suffer because of them?" I glared at Hans and Addie Marie, who were spooning into the gooey gray stuff like it was manna from heaven. They were so spoiled. Nobody did me any favors anymore.

"Not only do you have to suffer, Calla, but please do so in silence. And smile. I'd like our mornings to be as pleasant as possible before we all go our separate ways, thank you." Mom seemed to have forgotten that she'd asked about Logan and had gotten no answer. I should have felt lucky.

She leaned down, I guess to kiss me, but, too late, I slapped my spoon into my oatmeal in anger and a big gob flew up and landed next to her nose. We stared at each other. Feeling numb and empty, I watched her face turn beet red. Then she reached for a napkin to wipe the oatmeal off. The kids were giggling, but I could tell from Mom's expression that she didn't think it was funny. I didn't either, really. I waited for her to slap me, suddenly wanting her to, badly, but instead she walked to a chair and dropped into it.

"I'm sorry, Mom."

She didn't answer, just looked at me.

"Really, I'm awfully sorry. It was an accident."

For the longest time, she still didn't say anything. Then she shook her head. "Planting a blob of oatmeal in my eye maybe was an accident. But your brattish, childish behavior behind it was no accident. I'm trying to understand you, Calla. I'm trying to get along with you. But lately you're making it hard. Is there something wrong? Something bothering you? Do you feel well?" she asked in a half-exasperated, half-worried tone.

"Nothing's wrong, Mom. I'm okay." I couldn't meet her eyes, so instead I poured milk on my cold oatmeal and began eating it, fast.

"Good Lord, Calla, you didn't even put sugar on your oatmeal. That's normal?"

"It's okay," I said, but I knew what she meant. Besides fruit in my oatmeal, I like lots of sweetening, or spice. I can't swallow it plain, usually. I shrugged. I was on the verge of telling Mom what was wrong, but I just couldn't. Crying on her shoulder wouldn't bring Logan back, anyway. I did mean to stay out of further trouble, though. If I could. I was tired of feeling guilty and miserable.

With an exasperated sigh, Mom dropped the subject, but I could feel her still observing me right up to the time I left for school. I was glad to get away from her probing expression.

# eight

Emma and Rina were waiting for me when I got to school. I would rather have not been around them and their sunny-day attitudes, but how does a dog get rid of its tail? Between classes they trailed along, trying to cheer me up, although nobody came right out and said anything about Logan and me being finished.

At noon, they sat with their elbows practically in my macaroni and cheese, chattering on about bleaching tennis shoes. Rina had made a fuchsia pair pale pink and Emma had bleached her royal blue pair baby blue. Did they think I was so big a fool I didn't know we always talked about boys at lunch, things like how to get a guy interested in you? Bleaching tennis shoes! We did not discuss things like bleaching tennis shoes. When I got sick of it, I came right out and said, "I'm putting Logan out of my mind. Even if I have to cut my head off."

They both looked ridiculously relieved, I guess because I'd finally brought up the subject of Logan myself, not because I was going to guillotine myself if I couldn't forget him.

"Good idea!" Emma exclaimed, squeezing my hand. Rina put her hand on top of ours, smiling with moist eyes—and kind of cooing.

"But I don't know if I can," I said honestly. All three of us, I knew, were avoiding looking at Logan, who was eating lunch with Lawrie Stamper across the way. Earlier I'd seen her feeding him a carrot stick. They were so disgusting.

"I'll tell you what my dad says when he tries to talk me into breaking off with Shiney. I almost agree with him." Rina forced eye contact with me. "Dad says, 'There is more than one grain of sand on the beach.' "

I thought about that, but it sounded stupid to me—comparing sand with human relationships. I was ready to tell Rina how stupid I thought her dad was, but I caught myself just in time. After all, I was trying to stay out of trouble. Which reminded me: "Hey, I almost got busted for stealing a bra."

"You stole a bra, Calla?" Emma asked, wide-eyed with shock.

"No, I didn't steal one. This crazy clerk just thought I did." I went on to tell them the whole story. Which they loved, as I knew they would. And I knew that it would go into the annals of Treebrook Middle School oral history, too, now that I'd told Rina. I started stacking our empty dishes on my tray. I then asked my friends, "What does décolleté mean?"

Emma looked wise. "That's French. I think it means cut low, to show off your boobs."

I nodded. That described the big D bra I'd seen, all right.

"What did you think it meant?" Emma asked me.

"Pointy."

I stood up, ready to leave, so that I wouldn't have to look at Logan with Lawrie Stamper anymore, which was unbearable, although I was doing an admirable job of concealing how I felt, I thought. Emma motioned to me to sit back down, a funny look on her face, as though she were trying to get up courage to say something that was sticking in her throat. Reluctantly I sat down, but I turned my chair away from Logan's direction. "Hurry up," I told her.

She leaned toward us, very secretive, but she didn't look up. Instead, she started thumping this spilled piece of macaroni around on the table like she was playing marbles—strange behavior for Emmy. "This guy likes me and I don't know what to do," she said finally, tossing her blond hair but not looking at us.

"Who?" I demanded, afraid Logan was about to flea-hop to still another girl. "Who?" I repeated.

"Let her talk, for crying out loud." Rina looked threateningly at me before she twinkled excitedly at Emmy, "Tell us, Em."

Emmy took her sweet time, looking first at one of us and then at the other, her face getting pink—the most color I'd ever seen in it. Her pale freckles stood out like polka dots. "He's an egg-delivery man who comes by my folks' place—"

"Egg delivery man!" Rina practically shouted to the whole cafeteria. This time it was me who shushed her.

"He's nineteen, and he looks like Burt Reynolds, only not so smooth, kind of roughish," Emma blurted quickly.

"Sounds like a sleazo to me," Rina said.

I nodded, for once agreeing with her. But the truth was that I found the conversation boring. I'd thought, once I'd brought it up, that we'd be talking about Logan and me. It made me mad, now that I was ready to open up to them, that they were too insensitive to care, to see that I needed to talk and get rid of my frustrations. Who needed them, anyway? I'd brought up Logan before Emmy'd brought up this dumb romance of hers. "I gotta go," I said. I did a quick about-face as Logan and Lawrie, laughing, passed by me on their way out of the cafeteria, Logan so close that I could have reached out and touched his jeans. My throat closed with the old familiar hurt.

"Yeah, but what should I doooo?" Emmy pleaded.

Her babyish whine got to me. "Nothing!" I snarled at her. "You don't do anything, dummy. The guy's a sleaze and too old for you, besides. You've got a choice—tell 'em to get lost. Are you blind? You want somebody to draw you a picture?" Emmy stared, crushed. "Cal—?"

"You treat your friends just great!" Rina accused; she moved to stand by Emmy. "I don't know why we even bother with you, Calla. I don't think you want friends, anymore." She pulled Emmy to her feet and placed an arm about her shoulders.

I stood there for a long time, waiting to feel more human. "But—it wasn't—I do—" I sputtered, but I had waited too long. Rina and Emmy were halfway across the room. Escaping my poisonous aura, I guess. I didn't much blame them. At the same time, I was glad. It was too much trouble being nice, anymore, when I felt anything but. It'd be easier to be alone.

Yet, out of habit, I guess, I went to the senior citizen center that Saturday. Down deep I hoped my "grandmas and grandpas" could help me feel better. Leading their skits—doing small favors for them—had always made me feel better about myself. It was the last good thing I could count on.

When I got there, the center entry was bright and cheery as usual, but empty. Maybe I was very late and my old friends had given up watching for me. I lifted my wrist—unless my watch was wrong, I was on time. Even Mrs. Shawcross was not at her usual station in the gift shop.

Then, a burst of laughter and excited murmurs sounded from the main room. Why were they all down there, with no one to meet me? I tiptoed forward, my heart lifting when I realized I might be in for some neat kind of surprise. I needed one.

I was almost to the open double doors, the voices much louder, when Mrs. Shawcross's head popped around the door. "Calla!" she exclaimed, seeing me.

"Yes?" I hesitated.

"Would you watch the gift shop for a few minutes for me? In case someone comes in to buy something?"

"Um—sure." I wandered back to the corner of the entry sectioned off by counters. The space—wall, floor, and shelves—was packed with every imaginable handmade craft. I'd done some of my Christmas shopping here—crocheted pot holders and perfumed sachets for Mom, toy wooden puzzles for Hans and Addie Marie, and a plaque for Dad that read: LORD, GIVE ME THE STRENGTH TO GET ALONG WITH COMPUTERS!

I went around and sat on a stool, my feet curled

around the legs. For several minutes, I tapped a beatless tune on the edge of the counter with a pencil. Finding no thrill in that, I picked up a blue velvet pillow and paced back and forth, hugging it. If it was a surprise they were planning for me, I decided, I had to remember to act pleased, no matter how I felt.

I died of boredom three times before Mrs. Shawcross finally came huffing to the gift shop, a broad smile on her face. "Sorry," she said, "but I'm here now."

"What's happening?"

"Oh!" She clasped her hands under her chin, "Several of our people have been telling their experiences from their trip to Nevada this past week. They took the Fun Bus Tour to Reno!"

"Great," I muttered.

"Yes! It is wonderful when folks our age can still get out and have fun. Well, you may go now, Calla." She laughed. "No big rush of business while I was gone, I presume?"

I shrugged. "None." I added, not smiling, "But I made myself useful." I nodded toward a large Raggedy Ann doll sitting in a high chair. "She tried to elope with Andy, but I stopped them." The tone of my voice wasn't exactly friendly, either. Mrs. Shawcross looked at me as though she were wondering: Is this an honest joke and should she smile, or is this Calla Lea Stafford being sarcastic?

Give her ten minutes and she might get my drift, I thought irritably as I started down the hall to the main room. After all, she'd made me wait in the shop for a long time, for nothing.

The hubbub didn't mellow at all when I entered the main room. For a minute or two I just walked around, waiting for someone to notice that I'd come. Mr. Dabler spotted me and waved a bony hand but went right on talking to Thelma Merrill who, from the way she was carrying on, had to have been on that "fun bus."

"About our skit for the presidents' birthdays month—" I said in a loud voice, finally. "Don't you think we should get on with it?" The small groups about the room chattered on. That many of them weren't hard of hearing!

What was I—invisible? Had the rest of the world made up their minds, along with Logan, that I didn't exist? Well, I did—!

"All right!" I stormed to no one in particular. "If you don't need me here, I'll go home!" What was I doing here, anyway, while Logan was spending time with some other girl?

It came to me suddenly that the room had fallen silent; everyone was staring at me. My eyes smarted with sudden tears. "I'm sorry," I tried to smile, "I didn't really mean—"

"Oh, darling, it was us who were rude." Annie

Bybee hurried forward to clasp my arm. "We're the ones to be sorry."

"Everybody sit down!" Russell, already seated in his wheelchair, roared. "It's Calla Lea's time."

The others obediently found seats, except for ninety-nine-year-old Miss Jillian. She held her arm toward me, for me to walk her to a place on the couch. It was like I was frozen to the spot. When I finally lunged forward to help her, I almost knocked the frail woman down. I was falling apart, while more than anything in the world I wanted to hold myself together for these people.

I took my place in the center of the room to lead the discussion. "So—wh-what do you want to do?" I stammered. "Should we even have a skit this time? We skipped Lincoln's birthday—should we forget Washington's birthday, too?" I shifted to the other foot.

"Oh, I think such important days ought to be honored," Mrs. Edgerman offered, politely helpful. "Washington was the father of our country, after all. And Lincoln...we shouldn't be so busy that we pass up both days unrecognized."

"Maybe we can find a cherry tree and chop it down," Mr. Dabler chuckled.

I shook my head impatiently, feeling too harried and still on the edge, to give Dabler the laugh he wanted. Anyway, even nerdy Deanie Jones at school would know better than to make such a dumb remark. "Any other suggestions?" I frowned; my head was starting to hurt.

"I've been forcing some cherry branches into bloom," Mrs. Van Heusen offered. "We would have those to decorate with, if we waited a week."

"Can you force them to have cherries so we can have some pie?" Dabler guffawed, rocking back so far that I thought he'd tip his chair over.

He was worse than some of the kids at school! He was really getting on my nerves. When I brought my glance down from the ceiling, with a plea, "Be serious—!" I found him looking hurt and humbled, rocking slowly. He probably thought I had no sense of humor.

But at least he was being quiet. I nodded at Thelma, who was holding her hand in the air.

"Mr. Dabler's mention of cherry pie gives me an idea," she rasped. "Why don't we combine a real lunch with a skit? We can call it; 'George and Abe come to dinner,' or some such thing. If we hold it next Saturday, we'd have all week to get ready."

"A potluck," somebody said, "in costume!"

I heaved a sigh that the Reno fun trip was finally put to rest. Plans for a costume potluck dinner continued, generating excitement from most everybody. But, I had to admit, none of the good ideas were mine.

Later on, I was just glad to get out of the place, before I hurt any more feelings than I already had or created further dumb scenes. I'd had better days. A long time ago.

The next several days went by on about the same level—me being snappish to people even when I didn't plan to, friends and family pretty much steering clear of me when they could. I honestly didn't mind. I was getting to like being left alone. It was like I was in this big dark hole that I was digging deeper and deeper, and although it wasn't a great place to be, at least I didn't have to respond, didn't have to act happier than I felt.

One evening later in the week, I emptied a package of Sun-Corn tortilla chips down the disposal because they made me think of Logan. Listening to them grind away, I realized what I really could do about him. I could get even! I didn't know why I hadn't thought of it before. Why should Logan be so happy when I felt so awful? It wasn't fair! Sweet revenge—Yeah, don't get mad, get even—that was what I had to do!

Smiling, I shook the last of the chips into the disposal. Somewhere in the bowels of the thing, knives slashed and grumbled in the most satisfying way.

"I'm telling!" Hans roared suddenly in a voice far beyond his tender years. I hadn't known he was behind me.

"Telling what?" I pretended innocence, as if he'd seen nothing. My smile felt permanent.

He started to cry, "I'm telling Mom that you threw away the nacho chips she bought for Addie and me. Maaammaaa—" he wailed out of the kitchen.

I was only a little scared. Now that I'd made up my mind to get even with Logan, with only the how and where yet to be determined, I felt good enough to handle just about anything. And what was a dumb package of chips, anyhow? I'd buy the kids some Hostess cupcakes to replace them. I was having a glass of milk at the kitchen table when Mom, Hans, and Addie charged in.

Mom yanked out a chair and sat down in it. "All right, young lady, explain."

I looked at my mother; obviously the truth wouldn't make any sense to her. She had no idea of what I'd been through lately.

"Hans says you put a perfectly good package of corn chips down the disposal."

I nodded and had to swallow before I could talk. "You can't call them perfectly good..." I stalled for time.

"They were brand new! I bought them today!"

"Yeah, but they aren't good for people. Have you ever read the ingredients on the package, Mom? A lot of stuff most people can't even pronounce, strange stuff that could make us sick with cancer or—" I was really going good and hated for Mom to stop me, but she held up her hand.

"I don't buy it, Calla Lea. You guys would live on corn chips if I allowed it. Now, give me the real reason you threw them away?"

Everything about her voice and expression as she looked at me said that Mom meant business.

A new tactic would be desirable, but I couldn't think of any. It made me mad that my talent for making up stories should fail me at such an important time. I had to say something that would satisfy Mom, or I was really in for it. I probably was, anyway.

"I'm waiting."

"Mom's waiting," the little snots, Addie and Hans, echoed practically in unison.

"Just punish me, Mom," I said finally. "If you want a good reason why I did it, one that'll satisfy you, we'll be here all night. I just don't have one. You wouldn't understand—" I wasn't blind to the fact that I'd become like a crazy person. Mean, and a liar. But it wasn't intentional, really—

"You don't have a reason for destroying good food?" Mom looked at me head-on.

"Not such good food. It has—"

"Don't you dare start that again, Calla Lea Stafford." Mom threw me a murderous look. "You—!" The telephone rang there in the kitchen, interrupting her. I started to leave, but, like a finger of death, she pointed for me to stay right where I was.

I watched Mom try to regain her composure before she picked up the phone. "Hello? Oh, yes, hi, Mr. Dabler. How are you?" Her expression changed definitely for the better; a warm smile spread across her face. "Do we have any returnable pop cans or bottles you can clear out of our garage for us? Yes, yes, we do. No, no, I wouldn't think of it. You keep the money from them. It's worth it to me to have them taken out of my way. You hope the bag doesn't break like—when?" A look of puzzlement spread over her face then, her eyes widened, and her jaw dropped. "You saw her where?" she frowned. "When?" She looked over at me, ice crackling in her eyes. "I'm sorry about that. Yes. See you soon. Goodbye, Mr. Dabler."

"Go play in your room, kids," Mom motioned at Addie and Hans. "I have to talk to your sister, alone." The flat tone of her voice made me think of still, bluish-black air just before a storm. I cringed, my heart thumping, as I waited for the blast. I'd been caught. As sure as God made little red crab apples, Dabler had spilled that he'd seen me at the mall. Nothing had changed: Lies were still the world's worst gamble.

# nine

"Mr. Dabler says he saw you at Colburn's mall, around five o'clock, a week ago last Monday. He wanted you to help with some packages that'd broken open but you were too fast for him, didn't hear him call. And luckily, some friends of his came along. The mall, Calla, how about it? You told your father and me a real whopper about being held after school."

"I was at the mall."

"Why, when you know you're not to go there without permission?"

"I just wanted to go," I mumbled.

"And you lied to me about it, Calla. Why did you lie? Dad and I thought we could always trust you to tell the truth."

"I knew I'd get in trouble if I told the truth."

"You're in worse trouble now. Punishment is

definitely in order, don't you agree?" I refrained from shaking my head and just sat there. "You are grounded until further notice. And tomorrow, after you thoroughly clean that dump you call a room, you're to clean the garage. Clean it good! You can sort the bottles and have them ready for Dabler. While you're at it, I want you to do some good hard thinking about your behavior lately."

I protested, "Mom, tomorrow is Saturday. I have to go to the senior citizen center. They're counting on me. They're having a potluck dinner for Lincoln's and Washington's birthdays."

"Too bad you didn't think of that sooner." She looked at me for a long time, saying nothing. "I'm not sure I want to inflict you on those innocent people, the way you've been acting." She sighed. "But fulfill your responsibilities and, if there is still time, you can go. If you do go, call Mrs. Lakley before you leave, to stay with the kids. But you may go only to the center. For all intents and purposes, you're still grounded until I say otherwise."

"Grounded? Fulfill my responsibilities? Don't you mean serve my prison sentence?" I sobbed. "I'll never make it to the center. Cleaning the garage and my room will take all day. A week! They need me at the center. It's not fair to do this to them. I'm the one who got into trouble."

"Darn right you're in trouble. And they probably do need you. But the fact is, you'll do what I asked or not go at all. If you really care, Calla Lea, you'll manage it. While you're 'serving your sentence,' my little darling, please think over whatever is bugging you and then"— she looked at me not quite so mad, but seriously worried—"you're to come to me for a long talk. Do you understand?"

I understood. I understood plenty. Logan had done this to me, he was the cause of it all, and I would get him if it was the last act of my life.

Early the next morning, I dialed the senior citizen center, planning to explain that I would be late and might not make it at all. How I'd behaved the Saturday before was bad enough. I didn't want them to hold off their president's birthday celebration waiting for me.

I got a weird buzzing from the receiver and had to hold it away from my ear. Then, a quick call to the operator and I was told that the line was temporarily out of order but had been reported and was being fixed. With a sigh, I hung up the telephone, thought for a minute, then dialed Mabel Van Heusen's number. The ring jangled over and over while I agitated from one foot to the other. Treebrook's flower lady "extraordinaire" must be off somewhere, maybe outside in her yard.

I tried three more numbers with no luck. There had probably been a mass exodus from Conser

Arms to the center. I reminded myself that a lot of them did go early on Saturdays to spend the whole day involved in activities and visiting. The line to the center still wasn't working, and I was grounded until my penalty chores were finished so I couldn't leave to tell them in person.

I wanted to put the whole thing out of my mind, but then I thought there was a chance I might catch one of the old people walking by late to the center.

Maybe somebody I'd tried to call was just in the bathroom or something, hadn't heard the phone, and was now on the way to the center.

Nibbling my finger, I plunked myself down in Mom's rocker to watch out the living room window. Somebody better come along soon. I had to clean my room and then the garage, and I didn't care to be slaving until midnight. Of course, none of this would be happening if it weren't for that disloyal beast, Logan! I didn't know how I could ever have liked him, because I sure hated him now.

For several minutes I waited, rocking hard, tempted to throw things from frustration. If I was in this chair much longer, the kids would be perching on me to ask for a story. Luckily, the television had them captive at the moment. I used to be like them, though, believing a lap was mainly for holding a kid to tell a story. That was a long time ago. Today I wouldn't have minded being like a kid again. They'd grow up, too. And then Addie and Hans would know just how easy and nice it is to be a little kid, compared to the wretched mess called "adolescence."

I got up and went closer to the window and leaned my forehead against the cool glass for a while. Finally, I saw what I'd been waiting for. It looked like a bush moving up the sidewalk, but I knew it had to be Mabel Van Heusen, running late to the center with flowers and greenery for decoration. I raced out to the porch to wait until she got even.

Mabel spotted me. "See you later at the center," she called from around the huge bouquet she carried. "Better hurry, Calla." Unfortunately, she didn't slow down. For a second I couldn't move; I just watched the squat figure in a dull red coat and purple stocking cap move on down the street, branches of the bouquet looking like flowering antlers from the back.

"Mrs. Van Heusen—wait!" I raced to the end of our sidewalk and yelled again, "Just a minute, please, Mrs. Van Heusen. I have something I have to tell you!"

"Now?" She turned to peek at me around the bouquet.

"Yes, please." What I had to tell her would probably put the skids on her warm smile, and I felt lousy as I hurried up to her. "Mrs. Van Heusen, would you tell everybody I may be late today and they are to go ahead without me?"

"Oh, we can't get along without you, Calla. We're doing our special dinner today, remember? We're having speeches and cherry pie and everything."

What could I do? There was my term of punishment I had to serve. "I really can't help it, Mrs. Van Heusen. I'm sorry. But if—I can—I'll be there."

I didn't want to tell her that I was doing time for the crime of going to the mall, when I wasn't supposed to, and then lying about it. I shrugged, confessing, "I got into some trouble with my parents and I have some chores to do."

Mrs. Van Heusen frowned. "Well, I just don't know what we'll do without you, Calla. We could postpone the celebration, but it's really late for it already. Besides, these cherry blossoms won't last much past today. I've had these branches in water for weeks, forcing them to bloom. They wouldn't have bloomed naturally for six or eight weeks yet. I think the cherry blossoms are appropriate, don't you? For Washington's birthday, and all."

George would have approved. Abe would have liked them, too. "They're neat," I said. I reached out and touched a delicate white blossom. "I'd better not keep you any longer, Mrs. Van Heusen." I was using up my own time, too.

"My, no," she shook her head, starting off. "Bye, Calla. Now, you come today if you can."

"I will," I promised, watching her leave. If I killed myself working double-time I might get there. I was a slaving prisoner in my own home all on account of Logan McGee, a slimeball I was beginning to hate with a feeling more bitter than any I'd ever known.

I used the time that I dusted and vacuumed my room to consider the what's and wherefores of getting even with him. I could hardly wait to get back to school on Monday so I could make him cringe and crawl. In public. And I prayed he'd feel as bad as I'd felt seeing him talk to other girls.

The work went faster than I thought it would, I got so carried away thinking about sweet, soothing revenge. In the garage, while sorting bottles for Mr. Dabler to collect, I realized I could still get to the center before the party was all over. I really didn't want to go, though, when I thought about it. In the mood I was in, I hadn't been very pleasant at the center the week before, and I didn't want to dampen their celebration again. I had to finish this thing with Logan once and for all. The only way I could do that, plainly, was to hurt him like he'd hurt me. Then we'd be even. And I could get him out of my head.

I dawdled as I swept the garage and cleaned up a couple of grease spots. Even so, my conscience bothered me that I was letting my old friends down. I pushed the feelings aside and went up to my room when I was finished. For the first time in weeks, the top of my desk was clear enough that I could use it. I sat down and laid out a clean sheet of paper and a pencil. "Do unto Logan McGee as he has done unto me," I chanted to myself. "Do unto—"

At the top of the page I wrote: THINGS I CAN DO TO LOGAN. It was too late for the old "what's good for the gander is good for the goose" thing. Logan would probably be glad if I went out with other boys. He certainly wouldn't care, wouldn't be jealous if I did. No pain there. I nibbled on the pencil eraser.

Fifteen minutes later there were just two things on my list:

One:

Two:

Nothing more. It wasn't fair that my mind was a total abyss. I pounded the desk with my fist and heard sirens begin to scream at the same time, as if my banging had set them off. The wail came from east of us, in the direction of downtown. I'd grown out of hurrying to see the firetrucks go by, so I didn't pay much attention, except to note the crazy timing. Even when the trucks came shrieking up our street and on by, to turn the corner north onto Harlan, I didn't bother to go to the window. I just scratched my head and tried to think.

It struck me as really odd, though, when the telephone rang a few minutes later. Just two rings, so Addie, downstairs, must have answered it. I got a sudden sick feeling in my stomach. Mom was at the flower shop and Dad was at the post office doing some Saturday paperwork—safe—since both those places were in the opposite direction. But the senior citizen center—

I jumped a foot off the chair when Addie yelled, "Phone, Callie."

I lunged for my phone on the nightstand by my bed and snatched it up. "Hello?" I gasped.

"God, you took long enough!" Rina said breathlessly, "Listen, Cal, you know that place where you go all the time, the senior citizen place? It's on fire! I was just by there on the bus. I called because I was afraid you were there, this being Saturday. But Addie Marie said you were grounded and at home. I'm so glad. I thought, 'What if Calla is trapped and is burning up with those old people—' "

Somehow I managed to speak, although I felt turned to cold stone. "Rina. Thanks. Good-bye." I shook as I put the receiver back in place and then slid down to sit with my back against the wall, unable to stand on my feet. Not the senior citizen center! This shouldn't be happening to those dear, sweet old people, my friends. Behind my hands covering my face, I began to pray fervently: "Please,

God, help the firemen put out the fire, please, please!"

I had to do something. I had to see for myself if my old friends were all right. I would be in more trouble if I left the kids home alone than if I left and took them with me, I decided. We were going to the fire. "Addie, Hans," I yelled at the top of my lungs, "get your jackets on, quick."

I carried Hans on my shoulders, running most of the way, Addie's hand gripped so tightly in mine that she yelped and shook loose and just ran alongside of me, on her own.

We joined the watching crowd across the street from the center. I was sobbing now; I couldn't help it. Maybe if I'd made a real effort to be here earlier, there wouldn't have been a fire.

Actually, the center itself didn't look bad, although gray smoke still drifted up from the back where firemen trained their hose. I hadn't expected the building to be standing at all. On the way, I'd pictured an enormous pile of red coals. Some of the firemen were coiling other hoses, so I knew the worst was over. What bothered me was the fading scream of an ambulance that must have departed just before we arrived. I looked for familiar faces.

I saw Mabel Van Heusen right away, and Russell — wearing a hat like Lincoln's and wrapped in a blanket in his wheelchair, and, in an old-fashioned dress, Annie Bybee, whose true love story we had acted out for Valentine's Day. They huddled together like scared kids. Then I spotted Thelma Merrill only a few feet from me, in costume, too. I pushed my way through the people, dragging the kids, to where I could get her attention.

"Thelma?" my voice choked on a sob, "anybody hurt bad? The ambulance—" I couldn't say anything else.

For a second Thelma Merrill stared at me as if she didn't know me. Then she shook her head and grabbed me, holding me tight against her. "Calla, honey, it's awful. You weren't here today, were you? Thank God! You might have been hurt, too."

"But—who—was?" I managed to get the words out as she released me.

Thelma shook her head, and her eyes filled with tears. Her hands rubbed my arms up and down, up and down as she spoke. "Poor Mr. Dabler. Poor old Dabler, he got badly burned. They've taken him to the hospital."

"He'll be all right?" She nodded, but there was a question in her eyes. In emotional pain, I thought about Dabler, the many times I'd seen him stooping to pick up carelessly lost change in front of the tavern, his butter-and-egg money. I remembered all the times he'd lovingly teased me—at the center and other places—when I ran into him. Like the other old people, he'd been so good to me. Now this. He just had to be okay. "A-anyone else?" I gripped her hands, shaking all over as I waited for her answer, sure a lot of them were hurt because I hadn't been around to take care of them today.

She shook her head. "Just dear old Dabler." She finished in a husky, worried whisper, "I hope they're seeing to him in time. I pray he'll come out of this all right."

I nodded, feeling sick inside, yet numb. "What happened?" I asked. It helped that Addie and Hans were being quiet beside me, as they watched the firemen hurry back and forth, shouting directions to one another as they worked with hoses and hatchets. I couldn't have handled the kids otherwise, with my own feelings shattered and in turmoil. And, maybe this had had nothing to do with me. Maybe some of the elderly members had been making their homemade doughnuts and they'd had a grease fire in the kitchen, something like that. I tried to feel better, but I didn't. "What happened—how did the fire start?" I asked again.

"We were having such fun," Thelma told me, shaking her head, her voice huskier than usual. "Dabler was running the show. And loving it," she added. "He was dressed up as Washington. When you couldn't come, he said he might as well organize things for dinner. Of course, it was too much, but sometimes the rest of us sit back and enjoy ourselves while somebody else does all the work."

I couldn't say anything, as my mind filled with

further guilt. In heavy silence I watched as a few people started to leave. Beside me, Thelma shivered and drew her cape tighter about herself. It was quite a while before she went on. "Mr. Dabler passed Russell a thick lighted candle to take to the table, trying to help him feel useful, only Russell didn't have a hold on it yet and it dropped into his lap. The candle caught his lap robe on fire. Mr. Dabler saw what he'd done and snatched the candle and robe away, only then it caught his ruffled shirt sleeves on fire and the candle caught the tablecloth and then some curtains—That fire flared up so fast—"

She didn't say any more but I pictured the rest through the tears flooding my eyes. Like in a play, I saw the frightened old people trying to put out the fire on dear old Dabler, with someone hurrying as fast as he or she could—to call the fire department. Not many of them could move very fast. But I could have, if I'd been there. And I could have been. But I'd been too obsessed with plans for revenge against Logan; I'd chosen that over helping my friends. There mightn't have been any fire. If only—

Again I looked around and saw many of my elderly friends just standing around, dazed. They should go home. "Thank you, Thelma," I said, my throat tight with pain. I took the kids' hands in mine and walked over to the nearest old gentleman. "You should go home now," I told him. "It's over; everything will be okay now." I went from him to another, then another, each time being as comforting and calm as I could. I urged each of them to go on home and rest, promising that everything was going to be fine, even our dear Dabler, off at the hospital under doctors' care. I could only hope I was right. Gradually, they took my advice and started toward their homes in quiet, turtle-slow groups.

"They can rebuild the center," one old man hung back to tell me shakily.

"Sure they can, and they will," I reassured him.

I don't know how long the kids and I stayed, but it was until all the old people had gone. Later, we were walking up the sidewalk to our house as Dad pulled into the driveway in our blue Chrysler, home from work. I'd never been so glad to see anyone in my life, but for some reason, when he got out of the car, I didn't throw myself into Daddy's arms like I normally would. I told him what had happened and said that I had to go to the hospital to see Mr. Dabler.

He nodded, a concerned frown creasing his forehead. Inside, the kids went to their room to play fireman and Daddy went to the phone. I kept my eyes glued to his face as he talked. In a minute he hung up, giving me a relieved smile. "It's serious, but old Dabler is going to be okay. They want him to rest a few hours and then he can have a visitor or two. We'll go after dinner but only to stay a minute."

I nodded mutely, hoping I wouldn't be sick.

It was a waste of time to try and eat dinner, but I sat with the rest of the family and played with the egg rolls and shrimp on my plate—Mom had picked up Chinese food on the way home, hoping to cheer us up after Dad called her. Nobody said aloud that the whole thing was my fault. That if I hadn't gotten myself in trouble, then stayed home when I could have gone to the center, that the fire might never have happened. But they must have been thinking it. I was.

Later, standing by Dabler's bed, seeing his arms wrapped mummy-like in thick white bandages, his wrinkled old face scalding red and only a bit of his shaggy gray brows left, I could hardly keep from crying. "I'm sorry," I choked. "It's my fault you got hurt, Mr. Dabler. I'm so sorry." Like a fat white mitten, his hand reached for mine. "Nobody's fault," he mumbled through blistered lips. "Not yours, love. Accident."

Dad put his arm around me. "These things happen, Bright Eyes. You didn't do it."

I would have liked to have believed them, but of course it was my fault. And before mine, Logan's. And wherever he was, with whatever girl he was having fun with at the moment, it wasn't right that

Logan didn't know about the trouble he'd caused, to suffer with the rest of us. It wasn't right. He had to know. More than ever, I wanted to do something to shake him up. I wanted him to see that he couldn't hurt somebody, just walk away, and forget her. He couldn't just leave that person in so much pain that she hurt other innocent people, as I'd been doing so much lately. Logan needed to pay, along with me.

# ten

I wouldn't have guessed you could love someone so much and then end up truly hating them. Actually, I had heard of such a thing, but I would never have believed it of Logan and me.

It didn't help matters to see him first thing at school the following Monday morning, walking down the hall with still another girl, whose name I didn't even know. I was so furious that I could have scalped him and thrown his bloodied mop to a vampire for an appetizer! I could have beaten him to death with his old cowboy boots. I could think of a long revenge list now—!

Although I desperately wanted to do something bad to him, I was so mad I couldn't choose what actually to do. Nor could I think about classes or anything else. I just simmered inside as I went through the automatic motions of a school kid, opening and closing books, walking from one class to another. Then I saw him at lunch with the same girl and overheard them talking about horses. Horses! It seemed like the girl knew what she was talking about, besides, which was really unfair. That's when I got the idea to embarrass him, the idea I'd been looking for!

It was mid-afternoon and I was dying to go into action; I could think of nothing else. Before class started, I slipped into the art room after Mr. Huntley, the art instructor, went for his usual quick cup of coffee in the teachers' lounge. I closed the door and locked it after me. Working fast, because I didn't have much time, I found a wide paintbrush and some paint I knew was washable. On one wall with broad red strokes I painted:

LOGAN MCGEE KISSES HIS HORSE!!!

Logan's horse, El Cabrillo, which he'd had to leave behind in Texas, was as dear to him as a person. He wouldn't like being teased about his horse. Still, it wasn't enough. I thought about it, then painted on the next wall: LOGAN MCGEE IS A SELFISH IDIOT. I added:

L. M. KISSES SLEAZY GIRLS, BUT MOSTLY HE KISSES HORSES OR GIRLS WHO LOOK LIKE HORSES.

I'd used most of the wall space for my magnificent banners. I would have liked to draw some pictures, too, but there wasn't time. It looked great, anyway. I got rid of the brush and paint and ducked out of the room. There were kids churning in the hall but nobody seemed to notice me. I went to the restroom, smoothed my hair, and then fell in behind a bunch of other girls heading for art class. I looked for Logan, but he was lagging behind in the hall with that horsy girl, talking up a storm.

I watched the art room door open and heard a unified loud gasp from the group ahead of me. But it was Logan's reaction I wanted. "Where's Logan?" somebody screamed in the second of silence between the first gasping and the giggles that followed. "He's going to kill somebody!"

The tide of kids turned back out to the hallway, me caught among them, everybody but me motioning and yelling for Logan to come. He looked puzzled by the fuss, even a little worried. Around me, kids pushed and shoved. Some girl shrilled in my ear, "You gotta see, Logan. Wait'll you see!" I rubbed my ear, hoping my eardrum wasn't broken. I got out of the way as the crowd tried to squeeze into the room all at once. Over their heads I could see Mr. Huntley picking up speed way down the hall.

Everybody in the room got quiet as they waited for Logan's reaction. Trembling a little now, I watched his face as he read the first wall, the second, and the third. With each reading his face got darker. Then he just stood there, saying nothing. Loud laughter flowed into every corner of the room, just as I had wanted. "Hey, Logan," somebody snickered, "tell us about the girls. Tell us about kissing the horses."

"Yeah, horse lover," somebody else laughed, "you've been holding out on us. Tell us about horsing around with sleazy girls."

I'd have been elated, except that Logan just stood there doing nothing. The horsy girl put her hand on his arm. "It's a stupid joke, Logan. Don't pay any attention—" He yanked his arm away from her. "Well, excuse me!" she looked shocked, because he had been kind of rough.

"Hey, don't you know how to treat a girl?" Bryan Scott, who maybe had a thing for the girl himself, shoved into Logan hard from behind. Logan whirled and swung his fist at Bryan. Suddenly the whole room went crazy. Guys shoved and punched at one another, chairs crashed to the floor; girls screamed. I watched horrified. A fist came out of the melee and connected with Logan's nose. I saw blood spurt and witnessed the shock in his eyes from the sudden pain. Even though I hated him, I suddenly didn't want him hurt, not this way.

I jumped up on a chair and screamed, "Stop it! Don't hurt him. Everybody stop." Nobody could hear me—there was so much noise. I didn't see Mr. Huntley come in, but suddenly kids were freezing where they were, like in a game of statues. I realized all at once how scared I was, how weak and trembly, and I got down from the chair so I wouldn't fall.

Mr. Huntley looked at the paint on the walls, the tipped chairs, the scattered papers. Some of the kids started picking up books and righting chairs; others shuffled to their seats. I wanted to go to the restroom to get some paper towels for Logan. Then I saw Kristin LaSusa dig into her purse and hand him a packet of Kleenex. The bleeding had mostly stopped, anyway. Somehow, I got to my seat. I couldn't ever remember the room's being as quiet as it got then.

It was like I was in a nightmare, and I had caused every bit of it, only I couldn't believe I had. I felt cold and shivery, as though death had a hold of me. What had I done? What was wrong with me? Huntley strolled up and down the room studying each of our faces in turn, his own expression pure disgust. He went back to stand at the front of the room. "So, which of you is stupid enough to have pulled this stunt?" he asked.

I opened my mouth but nothing came out. Nobody else said anything.

"It's detention for the whole class if somebody doesn't speak up," Mr. Huntley warned.

I tried again, "I-I-did it." It didn't come out very loudly so I said, again, "I did it. This is all my fault."

Logan turned to look at me, but I couldn't see what was in his eyes. Rina and Emmy were looking at me, too, their chins practically on their desks. Mr. Huntley looked just as shocked. "Calla Stafford?"

I nodded. He looked like he still didn't believe me. He suspiciously eyed a couple of other kids—guys— known for making trouble. I held out my shaking hand to show him the red paint on it.

"Okay," he sighed, shaking his head. He looked at Logan and said wryly, "This is an obvious case of character defamation, if you care to pursue it in court." Logan, white-faced, kind of grinned and shook his head. A couple of kids snickered. I could have died.

"Calla," Mr. Huntley directed his stern voice to me, "this disruption and vandalism will have to be reported. I'm going to recommend that you wash the walls, in front of your peers. I doubt that you'll enjoy that." I shook my head, my face a furnace; tears filled my throat and welled into my eyes. "Then you will spend the remainder of the day in detention. Your parents will be called." I was barely aware of a couple of sympathetic moans, probably from my friends. There wouldn't be one from Logan. He must hate me now, horribly.

. . .

Sponging the walls with the kids', particularly Logan's, eyes on me was awful. It took a long, long time.

Worse was Mom's face when she came to the office where I'd been sitting on a chair until four o'clock, waiting for her to come and get me. As Mrs. Alsberg, our principal, repeated what I'd done, Mom kept looking at me as if I was someone else's kid. I wanted to apologize for being hers. But Mom reached for my hand when the principal went on with a speech about school rules that must not be broken, and about how I had always been a good student and that they hoped this was a one-time outbreak of mischievousness on my part. She hinted to Mom that maybe I had a problem of some kind that needed looking into. Mom hinted stronger that she agreed and would get to the bottom of the matter once and for all. She told Mrs. Alsberg that I would be punished at home, too. After that, we were free to go.

I was so ashamed that I could hardly look at Mom as we rode together in the car toward home. Neither of us said anything for a long time. Then Mom said, "Being thirteen isn't very easy, is it?" Her quiet voice brought a lump to my throat. "And being in love isn't all jolly fun, either," she added softly, looking at me. "I'm slow, Calla, but I've finally figured this out. It's about Logan, isn't it?

You two aren't seeing each other anymore, and you've been hurting?"

I nodded, the ache in my throat as big as a house. I hadn't expected her to understand and be this nice to me, and, though I didn't deserve it, I liked it. "Thanks," I mumbled. As my tears erupted, I moved over and put my head on her shoulder. When I could talk, I told her about Trinket and Logan's coming to my table at Happy Hank's, how much I'd liked Logan from then on, how wonderful it had been. Then, suddenly the Valentine's note saying it was over. Mom just listened, with one hand on the wheel and the other around me. Once she squeezed me and said, almost crying herself, "It's important to get the hurt all out, Callie, so you can get on with life."

She couldn't have been more right, I began to realize. Talking to her still later at home, helping fix dinner, I'd never felt closer to her. It made me think of the old days when I was little and talked to her all the time. Of course, breaking off with Logan was very different, so personal.

"Mom, I did the stupidest things. I knew when I did them that I was being crazy but I just couldn't make myself stop." She already knew, from the school, about the signs. Now I told her the truth about the lemons, what I'd really wanted them for. Mom laughed and said she used to do things like that when she was thirteen.

I told her about the makeover that didn't get finished, my brush with the law over the bra, the snits I'd gotten into with my friends. I shut up for a minute and then I said, "You know, it kind of felt like I was— do you really think I—?"

She took my chin in her hand. "No, darling, you didn't actually lose your mind. You responded like any normal person might, who was enduring a lot of pain. A little odd, maybe, but definitely not true bats."

"I love you, Mom."

"You, too, Babe."

I wished I had talked to her earlier, before I'd made such a fool of myself, and before I'd caused other people to get hurt. After dinner, I sat between Mom and Dad on the couch. Addie Marie, hovering, asked, "Is Callie sick?" She kept staring at my red and swollen eyes.

"Does she have a pain in here?" Hans patted his stomach.

"I used to, only higher," I answered him with a hug. "But it's going away." I wiped at my nose, which had begun to tingle with one last unshed tear.

"Calla's fine," Mom assured them.

"She just needs some extra loving," Dad added.

Addie Marie and Hans took Dad at his word. They threw their crunchy-soft bodies on me and began planting wet kisses all over my face. Before I could hold them off, Dad began to tickle me and Mom helped until all of them had me laughing my head off. It was like I was getting back to solid, familiar ground after an eerie trip into space or somewhere.

"I don't ever want to fall in love again," I told Mom later.

"Oh, yes, you do," she said. "Hon, there's always a risk when we fall in love, the risk that the other person might not love us back as much. You may avoid some suffering, if you don't take that risk, but you'll also have nothing. Just nothing. You won't learn, or feel, or change and grow. And you won't find that one person who will love you deeply in return, if you don't take the chance."

I thought about that quite a bit the next few days. Being grounded doesn't have a lot going for it, but it does give you a chance to think. At school, I studied Logan, but in a different way. It struck me that he didn't look like the same boy, that young cowboy who showed up in Treebrook during Christmas break. In just a couple of months he'd come to look like the other guys.

People sure changed. Or maybe he never was that boy I'd fallen in love with—maybe that boy was just a fantasy. A dream of my heart not meant to last, but rather to become part of my experiences, part of me. I knew now that if—no—when I fell in love again, I'd do things differently. I'd know that all relationships aren't necessarily meant to last forever but are just to be enjoyed for the time. I'd know that breaking up hurts, but doesn't kill a person.

It was maybe three or four days before I looked out our front window one afternoon and saw Logan sitting on our front porch. My heart gave a lurch and I wondered if he was "back" back. Then I knew it was all over and he'd probably come to bawl me out, putting it off as long as he was able. He'd probably built up a real head of steam. Well, I had it coming.

"Logan's out there," I told Mom, who was watching me curiously from the chair where she'd been sewing a button on Hans's overalls. "Should I talk to him?"

"Why not?" she smiled. "It might be a good idea to get everything out in the open and settled once and for all. But remember, Cal, no matter what you two say to each other, keep in mind that you're a great kid, because you are." She grinned and motioned toward the front door. "And so is he."

I nodded and heaved a deep sigh. I didn't feel the least bit scared as I went out and sat down next to Logan. In fact, I felt very calm and good. He was the one who looked worried. I gave him a chance to start, but when he didn't say anything I guessed it was for me to apologize. "I'm sorry about the stuff I wrote on the art room walls, Logan. I've been jealous and that's why I did that asinine thing. Other stupid things. I've been pretty mixed up."

He kept rubbing where his jeans stretched over his knees. Finally he said, "I know you did it because I hurt your feelings. I knew it right away, as soon as I saw that writing. I've been too chicken to come and tell you, but—I really didn't blame you."

"You didn't? Don't?" That surprised me.

He shook his head. "I think I kind of flaunted the other girls, not caring enough about your feelings. My dad was like that. That's part of the reason he and Mom split. I've been thinking about Dad a lot, now that spring break is almost here and I'll be going to spend some time with him." He added slowly, "I wouldn't admit it to myself before, but I think I always knew Dad liked playing around and didn't care who he hurt. Until I saw what you'd done in the art room, I hadn't realized I was behaving just like him. I'm sorry, Callie."

I could see that he really meant it and felt bad. "It's all right," I said.

He asked, "Honest? What did the office say? I know you didn't get suspended, but will they put it on your record or anything?"

I shook my head. "They figure that I just flipped out this once and that it won't happen again. Because I've never given them any trouble before they didn't suspend me, but I am on probation for a while."

A look of relief showed in his hazel-green eyes and he nodded. "Good. And your parents, what did they say?"

"Well, I am being punished," I told him. "Mom tells me now that as a surprise I was supposed to get to go to Seattle and visit my cousin over spring break, and now I can't go. I have to stay home and help with the spring housecleaning instead. Considering, they've been pretty neat. I guess I got off lucky."

We sat quiet for a while and then I told Logan, "I thought you came over to yell at me."

"No." He shook his head, grinning as he looked away from me. He cleared his throat. "I came because—because I was sorry. And I wanted you to know I still think you're one of the neatest girls I've ever met. We had a lot of fun; you made coming here to Treebrook easier for me. I still like you very much." He turned to look at me, his expression more serious. "But I still think we are too young to get serious and never do anything with other people. I like girls, other girls, and going around with them, but when I do, it doesn't mean I don't like you. I want you to understand that, Cal, and I should have made it more clear before."

"It's all right. I think you're neat, too, Logan."

Then I added quickly, so he wouldn't think I'd gone off the deep end again, "...as a guy, a friend."

He sighed and looked up at the tree branches over our heads, where fat leaf buds were beginning to show. "Winter's almost over," he said.

"Yeah," I agreed. February—"month of hearts and flowers" as Annie Bybee called it—was gone. March was blowing in fresh new winds. "You have a good time in Texas, Logan," I told him.

"I'll be back," he said.

We looked at each other. I laughed, although I couldn't have said why. Then Logan laughed. Our laughter rose and swelled and bound us warmly together. Only in my heart did I look at him one last time in "that way."

Because I had surely loved him, Logan McGee.

## *a look at: run from a scarecrow*

***What's the secret that keeps Hank's mute friend on the run? And who is the strange man that follows them out west?***

In the 1880s, young Hank's dream of moving west and becoming a cowboy is hindered by his responsibilities to his family. But he makes friends with a mute boy who has a secret, and helps protect him from the scarecrow man that tracks them both down.

Hank's friend surprises everyone by speaking, after years of silence—and then revealing his family's secret.

**Follow this young frontier hero in a wild adventure rich in mystery and suspense from award-winning author Irene Bennett Brown. Get your copy now and dive into a world brimming with suspense, discovery, and the resolute spirit of the frontier!**

*AVAILABLE NOW*

# about the author

Irene Bennett Brown is an award-winning author who enjoys using Kansas—where she was born—as background for her historical novels. Previous to her ten novels for adults, Brown authored nine young adult novels. *Before the Lark* won a Western Writers of America Spur Award, was nominated for the Mark Twain Award, and received other honors. Her other YA novels include *To Rainbow Valley, Run from a Scarecrow, Skitterbrain, Willow Whip, Morning Glory Afternoon, Answer Me Answer Me, I Loved You Logan McGee, and Just Another Gorgeous Guy.*

Her most recent Nickel Hill series include *Miss Royal's Mules, Tangled Times, Somebody's Business* and *One True Deed.* All are adult sequels to *Before the Lark.*

She lives with her husband, Bob—a retired research chemist—on two fruitful acres along the Santiam River in Oregon.

Visit her website at irenebennettbrown.net for more information.

www.ingramcontent.com/pod-product-compliance
Lightning Source LLC
La Vergne TN
LVHW030921080826
845145LV00013B/2996

* 9 7 8 1 9 5 7 5 4 8 8 1 4 *